A BOX OF NOTHING

When James slipped through the fence into the Dump, it had been almost pure impulse. His idea was to find the box of nothing, hide it and then pick it up later.

But it wasn't there. Instead, James saw a mauve and yellow cliff. It was a long way up the slope, further than from home to school, more than a mile. Frightened, he swung back to scramble through the fence and get away.

But the fence had gone . . .

PETER DICKINSON
A Box of Nothing

Illustrated by Ian Newsham

A Magnet Book

First published in 1985 by Victor Gollancz Ltd
This Magnet paperback edition first published 1987
by Methuen Children's Books Ltd
11 New Fetter Lane, London EC4P 4EE
Text copyright © 1985 Peter Dickinson
Illustrations copyright © 1985 Ian Newsham
Printed in Great Britain
by Richard Clay Ltd, Bungay, Suffolk

ISBN 0 416 96630 6

Contents

Chapter 1

THE NOTHING SHOP

There was nowhere to hide. Mum had just turned the corner out of Floral Street and she only didn't see James because she was shouting over her shoulder at Angie to hurry her up. The gold September sunlight glittered off the shafts of the pram. Mum stood there, round as a jug because of the next baby, and the twist of her head to yell at Angie and the push of her body to hold the pram gave her a look of fighting her way into a wind, though there wasn't a whisper of one in the long, empty road. In a couple of secs she'd look round and see James.

Opposite him lay the Borough Dump. Kevin at school said there was a loose bit of the fence where you could slip through, but James didn't know where it was, and anyway Mum would be bound to spot him dashing across the road and then it would be worse still. There were swarms of rats in the Dump, Mum said, and you could get Weil's disease from rats, whatever that was.

This side of the road there were only the blank brick walls of warehouses, and between them, just where James was standing, the Nothing Shop. James flattened himself into its doorway. She'd see him when she came past, of course. He'd have to think of a story.

He couldn't make thoughts begin. Instead he stared across the road at the sunlit mounds of rubbish above the iron fence. If he half-closed his eyes so that his eyelashes blurred things he could make the mounds into a great range of mountains, miles away, streaked with snow and glaciers where the white enamel flanks of cookers or dishwashers made part of the slopes. The scavenging gulls became enormous—huger than eagles they'd have to be for him to see them from so far off. He blurred the scene a bit more and the rusty iron fence became streaky and stretched out into a sort of iron sea between the road and the mountains . . .

It was no use thinking of a story. Mum wouldn't believe him. He could hear them now, Mum's scolding quack at Angie and the gargle of a twin pretending it could talk and the twitter of the loose pram wheel. Best thing was to jump out and shout "Boo!" and pretend he'd been hiding there for that.

He leaned against the door, tensing for the ambush.

Behind him he heard a click. The door moved. It creaked. It was open.

He twisted, slipped through and closed it behind him.

It was just what he'd imagined inside. Windows so filthy that they turned the sunlight grey. A bare counter, with empty shelves behind it. Dust, cobwebs, silence.

It wasn't really called the Nothing Shop—that was just the name he gave it in his mind. The writing on the board over the door was so flaked you couldn't read it. Ages ago, Dad said, there used to be streets of little slum houses where the Dump was now, too grotty to be done up the way Floral Street had been. So they'd all been pulled down and no one used the road except a few families taking the short cut to school, and the rubbish-trucks. There was no one for the Nothing Shop to sell things to, so it just stood there waiting for the Dump to be cleared away and made into a park, like the Borough Council kept promising.

James was poised by the door with his ear against the crack so that he'd know when Mum had gone past when

8

he heard, behind him, a creak. He froze. Soft footsteps slithered. A floor-board creaked again.

"Yes?" said a quiet voice.

He forced himself round. The man behind the counter looked old, and dusty as the shop in the grey light, but not actually doddery. He wore a dark grey dust-coat and peered at James over the lenses of tiny half-moon spectacles.

"And what can we do for you, sir?" he said.

"Nothing," said James.

"Any special brand of nothing?"

Mum's Dad was like that, always picking up things you'd said and giving them meanings you didn't mean. James knew how to play.

"Best you've got," he said. "Looks as if you've got plenty."

The main raised a spidery grey hand and ran it up the bald strip above his forehead.

"Not much call for quality these days," he said. "People don't seem to have the time."

"I only want the best. Not that ordinary stuff on those shelves."

"Well now, we'll have to see."

The man reached under the counter and pulled out a thing like a wooden chair, but when he tilted the top over it became a short step-ladder. Gripping the shelves to steady himself he climbed to the top step, then began to grope around on the highest shelf. He grunted and climbed back down.

"Knew we had a bit left somewhere," he said.

He put on the counter a square box, only a couple of inches across, made of thick old brown cardboard. When he blew the dust off it James saw the letter O stencilled on the lid in purple ink. Probably the Nothing Shop used to sell boxes, along with stationery and other things, and Size O was the smallest one.

"How old are you then, sir?" said the man.

"Ten and a bit," said James.

"And how old is the world, would you imagine?"

He must have been watching the same TV programme as James, only last night, all about the Big Bang, and Black Holes, and quasars, and other stuff James thought specially interesting and Mum thought specially pointless and boring.

"Four and a half billion years," said James.

"Near enough for practical purposes," said the man. "What about the universe, then?"

"They're still arguing."

"Taking their time, aren't they? Long enough to think it out, considering."

"Anyway there was this big bang and it all went whoosh and started."

"Right. And before the bang, what?"

"Nothing. No space. No here or there or anywhere. No time either. It doesn't make sense, but that's what they say."

"All right. Now what we have here, young sir, is a bit of that original nothing. Very best nothing there's ever been. You're lucky to find us still in stock. Been no call for it, not for donkey's years, like I was saying."

"How much?" said James.

The man picked up the box and peered at the bottom.

"Must have been in here a good few years," he said. "Nought pounds, nought shillings and nuppence— what's that in new money?"

"Nought pounds no p."

"There you are, then."

James dug his hand into his jeans pocket, took out an imaginary purse, mimed it open and counted some pinches of air into the man's palm.

"Thank you, sir," said the man. "Will that be every-thing?"

"Yes, thank you."

As James picked the box off the counter the man pressed

the keys of an invisible till. He was good. He almost made James think he heard the ping of a bell as the imaginary drawer slid open. He counted the money into separate compartments and slapped the drawer shut.

Although it was only cardboard the box had a good solid feel to it. Even if there was nothing in it it wasn't the sort of rubbish people give away for a joke. James turned towards the door, expecting to be called back. He would have liked to keep the box. It was interesting. For one thing there didn't seem to be any way of opening it. He turned it over and looked at the bottom. There was something written there in pencil, spidery slanting figures —£o. os. od. But that meant . . .

He looked over his shoulder. There was nobody behind the counter.

Chapter 2

THE FENCE

Mum was slap outside on the pavement. It was sheer bad luck—she hadn't spotted him trying to hide and waited, but Angie had skipped a shoe off and Mum had stopped to put it on. She'd got her glove in her mouth to tie the knot so she wasn't quacking, and the twin had stopped gargling because they did sometimes, and the pram wasn't being pushed so there was no twitter from its wheel. No warning at all.

"James!"

"Hello, Mum."

"What are you doing here?"

"Nothing."

"Why aren't you at school?"

"I don't know."

That wasn't true. He was late for school because he was frightened of Mrs Last, having to explain to her he still hadn't found a seed and drawn the picture of the plant it grew from. The first homework that term. Supposed to be an easy one to start with, only it wasn't James's sort of thing. Yesterday he'd told Mrs Last he'd left it at home. Everyone else had brought theirs—an ear of barley and a drawing of a barley-stalk, an acorn and an oak, a hip and a rose-bush, a coconut and a palm, even. No problem, only James's pictures always came out somehow messy.

He'd actually started on a conker-tree picture last night

and he'd been going to pick up a conker on his way to school from the tree growing just inside the Dump fence, only there'd been the TV programme about Black Holes and things and he'd tried to draw and watch at the same time and made even more of a mess than usual and now he couldn't even find a conker in the road because the rubbish trucks had squashed them all, so . . .

"What's that you've got?" said Mum.

"Oh, nothing."

"What do you mean, nothing? Only word you know, is it?"

"It's a box of nothing. The man gave it to me."

"What man?"

(You mustn't talk to men you didn't know, specially not let them give you things.)

"In there."

Mum frowned at the shop. Of course she'd seen it before, hundreds of times, but she wouldn't have really looked at it, or wondered. It wasn't her idea of an interesting place—old, filthy, silent, strange.

"He's the shopkeeper, I suppose," said James. "I mean he was wearing a sort of coat like they do. He gave me a box of nothing and I gave him nuppence for it. It's only a joke, Mum. Like Grandad's."

It was a mistake bringing Grandad in. Mum was fond of him, of course, but he fussed her, like a picture she couldn't get to hang straight.

"Well, you're going right back in and giving it back to him," she snapped, "or I'll be giving you something. Quick now. I haven't got all morning."

James sighed and turned. At least it had taken her mind off him being late for school. The door wouldn't budge. He put all his weight against it, but he could tell from the feel that it wasn't just locked. It was shutter than that, bolted top and bottom, nailed through, hinges rusted fast, spider-webs across the cracks. But he'd . . . And Mum had seen him coming out, hadn't she? No she hadn't, because she'd been doing Angie's shoe. A twin started to whine.

"Thought so," said Mum. "Nobody opened that door to my knowledge these ten years. I'm beginning to think you've got too much imagination for your own good, my lad. Picked it up in the road, didn't you?"

(That was another rule. You didn't pick things up, specially in this road where they'd probably fallen off one of the trucks, which meant they'd come out of someone's dustbin.)

"Hand it over, then," said Mum.

James longed to refuse. There was something really strange about the box, and the price on the bottom, and the man in the shop, and the door which really had been open a few minutes back. But Mum was always too strong for him, too certain what she thought and wanted. It was as if her mind, not his, made his arm reach out and opened the grip of his fingers so that she could take the box. She locked the brake of the pram and strode with her pregnant waddle into the middle of the road. James got his own will back and scampered after her.

"Oh, please, Mum . . ."

She swung her arm back and bowled the box, round-arm, over the fence. It seemed to float as it flew, sunlit against the pale sky, before curving down to join the rest

of the rubbish. Without noticing what he was doing James took a few paces after it. It fell out of sight just below an old broken kitchen cabinet painted a horrible yellow and mauve.

There was a rumble down the road. Two refuse trucks had turned the corner out of Floral Street, loaded with the throw-outs of hundreds of houses. They churned up towards James. Mum had turned back the moment she'd slung the box and was already on the pavement, looking to see where he'd got to.

"James!" she screeched. "Wait! Get back! Stay that side! Right against the fence!"

He trotted forward and flattened himself against the corrugated iron. Waiting for the trucks to pass he glanced down at the strip beside him and saw that it was half-loose. The nails that held the bottom and the middle had fallen out or had been pulled out and it was only hanging from the top. Slipping his hand between it and the one behind he found he could sway it outwards a few inches. Then it stuck because the one beyond overlapped it and held it firm.

The first truck came grinding past. James hesitated. The moment the second one hid him from the far pavement he crouched right down, tugged the iron sheet as far as it would go and scraped himself through the slit. The fence clashed back into place before the truck was past.

Vanishing trick, he thought. That'll teach her for chucking my box away like that. Now . . .

He straightened to look for his landmark, the yellow and mauve cabinet half way up the rubbish-pile. What he saw was something quite different.

When James had slipped through the fence it had been almost pure impulse. His idea, if you could call it that, was to find the box and hide it just inside the fence, and then pick it up on his way back from school. He wouldn't tell Mum, though. He'd just pretend it was a quick tease for chucking his box away. She'd go mad, of course, and rabbit on about the rats and Weil's disease, but it wouldn't last. She was always too busy with the next thing to stay angry for long about the last one. And it ought to be easy to find the box with that horrible cabinet to go by. But it wasn't there.

Instead, James saw a mauve and yellow cliff. It was a long way up the slope, far further than Mum could possibly throw, further than from home to school, which meant more than a mile. Frightened, he swung back to scramble through the fence and get away.

The fence had gone. Its colour was still there, and some of its shape, but changed and stretched out flat and enormous. James was standing on the shore of an iron-grey sea, flecked with patches of rust-colour, and covered with very regular small round waves. It stretched away and away towards the skyline. From beyond that unreachable horizon his name was being called. He couldn't hear it, but he could feel it.

Chapter 3

THE DUMP

A stream flowed down from the mountain. It was a real mountain, but there was something wrong with it, not just that there didn't seem to be a tree or a bush or a blade of grass anywhere, but something else. There was something wrong with the stream, too. A little way up the slope it flowed over a ledge into a pool, and James could see that the water—if it was water—was a bright browny orange. Blobs of yellow foam floated on the pool, and the surface between them shimmered with rainbow colours.

All along the shore of the iron sea, like a sort of high-tide mark, was a line of ordinary rubbish. James picked his way through it and started to climb the slope. The ground was a jumble of rocks, with soft places between, but the rocks were funny shapes. James stared at one, puzzling what was wrong with it, and suddenly saw that although it looked and felt like an ordinary seaside rock it had once been something else, some kind of machine, part of a record-player set perhaps, which had turned into rock somehow and then got worn at the corners. The whole slope was like that, made of people's throw-outs which had turned into rocks. Gone fossil. The soft places between crunched like breakfast cereal when he trod there. The whole mountain had once been rubbish. It was high enough for its peak to be streaked with snow.

Three enormous white birds were circling round the peak with the slow, drifting flight of gulls.

When he'd climbed far enough to see over the fence, supposing the fence had still been there, James turned again. He knew it wouldn't work, but he couldn't help hoping that from up here he would be able to see that it really was only a fence, and Mum would be there on the pavement in front of the Nothing Shop, yelling at him to come back. But all he saw was the sky, and the vague horizon, and the iron ridges of the sea. He shut his eyes and counted slowly to twenty before he opened them, but he still couldn't make the fence come back. What's more it wasn't going to, not until he found his box of nothing. All this had something to do with that. It was obvious. And he would never get home without it.

So he turned his back on the sea and climbed on, scrambling up the fossil rubbish. It wasn't difficult or dangerous, but it was hard work. Whenever he stopped for a rest he checked on the birds. They really were gulls, he decided, even though they were far too big. But then everything was too big. Down on the shore the rubbish had seemed sort of normal, but up here things, where he could recognise them, were enormous. The cupboard he was aiming for had become a great cliff. A fossil shoe was a yard across . . .

Or had he become small? He didn't think so. If you shrank that much all your veins and things would shrink too. They'd become much too thin for the blood to get through. Dad had explained about that when they'd been watching an SF film about doctors being made tiny to go and put something right inside somebody's body. Anyway, James felt perfectly ordinary, apart from being frightened.

There were two kinds of fright—fright at the strangeness and the lostness, and fear of the gulls. The gulls were bigger than eagles, as big as aeroplanes. He thought of gulls at the seaside. They have a mean look and they snap things up. These ones were big enough to snap up a boy if they glided this way and spotted him scrambling over the rocks. There was nowhere to hide on the bleak slope. He'd better be quick and find that box.

Hurrying enough to make himself pant he came to a place where the slope levelled out into a flat, grey space as big as a football pitch. The cliff he was aiming for was a bit further up the slope on the far side of it. It really was a cliff, far too big to have been a cupboard, but still the mauve and yellow it had been painted when it hung in someone's kitchen. The yellow was rock, and the mauve was some kind of streaky stain. Half way between the grey patch and the cliff lay a white box. From this distance it looked like a perfectly good fridge, only for some reason it hadn't gone fossil, like everything else. Funny.

The grey patch had a greasy, sticky look, but at least it was flat. James was just going to step out on to it when in front of him it rose into a hummock. The hummock swelled until it was almost a yard across, then a hole appeared in the top and it collapsed with a whistling sigh and a plop. Plus a really foul smell. All across the patch the same thing was happening, sigh, suck, plop, like an enormous pan of porridge boiling. It wasn't going to be much use looking for the box if it had fallen anywhere in that mess. He began to pick his way round the edge.

Half-way round he came to a path which ran along the edge of the porridge lake for a bit and then slanted up the slope below the cliff. A path meant people. Or things. James wasn't sure he wanted to meet anyone in this strange place, but the path was going the way he wanted, and besides it seemed to be getting dark. Yes, the sun was low and the sky that way was all pink and gold, although James could still taste the cleanness in his mouth from brushing his teeth after breakfast, only an hour ago.

He was striding up the path, looking to left and right among the jumbled rocks because he was getting near the area where he thought the box should have fallen, when his leg caught in something. He staggered forward and grabbed at a rock by the path to stop himself falling. Then he felt the pain in his shin.

"Ouch!" he said, though there was no one around to hear.

He stood on one leg, rubbing his shin and looking to see what had tripped him. Nothing. Oh, yes, a trail of loose wire. It had been stretched across the path on purpose to trip people and he'd bust it by walking into it so hard. Stupid idea of a joke. He limped on.

The path ran close by the white box he'd seen from the other side of the porridge lake. It was a fridge, no use any more because of its door being loose. Why hadn't it gone fossil and huge, like everything else? Perhaps one of the gulls had picked it up on the shore and dropped it here, the way ordinary gulls do with mussels and things, to bust it open and get at the food inside. Still, just because it was different James decided to have a look.

The box of nothing was lying against the back of the fridge, wedged between it and an upside-down tin bucket with its bottom rusted out. The bucket hadn't gone fossil either. James picked the box up and turned and looked at the sea. It was still there. No different. Perhaps when he got back down to the shore . . .

He glanced towards the sunset to try and guess how long he had before it was dark. There, black against the gold-tinged sky, floated three great winged shapes. The gulls were coming.

James stuffed the box into the pocket of his anorak and crouched down. It wasn't any use. They'd spot him from miles away in his blue jeans and scarlet anorak, the only blob of colour on the grey mountain slope. The gulls weren't hurrying, in fact as James watched them, wondering what to do, he saw them circle back and right round before gliding on. They must be actually trying to slow down. They weren't interested in James yet, because they were interested in something underneath them. Something moving this way.

Something or someone had put a trip-wire on the path. Better not stay so close to it.

Still crouching, James squirmed and scrabbled his way up to the foot of the cliff. There might be a rock there, leaning against it, making a little cave he could wriggle into. Something like that. But there wasn't.

The gulls were getting closer. They'd pretty well certainly spot him if he tried to scuttle away along the foot of the cliff. Spot him if he stayed, too.

As he huddled himself against the cliff, watching the approaching gulls, a new feeling came over him, a sort of shrinking chill and stillness. Somebody or something was watching *him*. Close, close by.

He managed to force his head round. A crack had opened in the yellow rock. In that narrow slot of dark something glistened, a curving gleam, the lens of a large eye.

"We thought we felt an alarm go off," said a voice. "The patrol will be along in a minute. You had better come inside."

It was a machine voice, the sort that computers talk with.

"I'm all right," said James.

"Until the patrol finds you," said the voice. "We strongly advise you not to allow that to happen. In fact, we insist."

The slit widened. A furry yellow arm with no proper fingers came through, took James gently by the elbow and pulled him into the dark.

Chapter 4

RAT PATROL

The rock closed and the arm let go. James wasn't as frightened as he might have been, because what he'd been really afraid of was the gulls and whatever they were following along the path, and he was safe from them now. But when he looked at his rescuer his heart jumped.

There was only a faint pale light from somewhere overhead, so it wasn't easy to see, but the thing standing in front of him certainly wasn't human. It didn't look like a proper animal either, or if it was one it must have had some kind of terrible accident. It stood on its hind legs like a human, but its head was more like a donkey's with two long ears and a muzzle. One huge eye gleamed in the dim light. The body was a shapeless lumpy bag wearing what looked like a sailor's shirt. One arm was short and stubby and the other long and thin. The legs were in shadow, but they didn't seem to match either.

"How do you do?" said the computer voice, spacing the words out.

"Hello," James managed to say. "I'm James."

The creature paused.

"Call us Burra," it said. "Yes, the Burra. We are the Dump Burra."

It sounded as though it had only just decided what its name was.

"What did you mean about the patrol?" said James. "I saw some gulls."

Again there was that slight pause.

"Rats," said the Burra. "You must have set off one of their trip-wires. Come and see. This way, if you please."

In a lop-sided, clumping walk it led the way across what seemed to be a small cavern. The dim light came from a short length of tube poking out of the far wall. Just below the light a door opened before the Burra reached it. Beyond was a flight of stairs, much more brightly lit because the tube ran the whole way up. As he climbed them James saw that he'd been right about the Burra's legs—they weren't just different lengths, they were different kinds. The right-hand one belonged to a camel or something, but the left one was human, except for being made of wood. It had a proper knee and ankle and foot, and a shiny black dancing shoe. It clumped on the stair-treads. The same with the arms. The furry one came off a teddy bear, but the other was thin and green and had three fingers so it must have belonged to a Kermit. In fact the Burra was somehow made of a lot of bits of different toys.

As they went up the stairs the light came too, coiling along like a tame luminous worm overhead. The Burra led the way into another cavern, much larger than the one below, with patches of twinkling small lights here and there and full of mild hums and whirrings. The light-tube coiled along the roof, tied itself into a knot and let down a loop of light over a table in the middle of the floor. The Burra clumped across to the far wall of the cavern.

"Come and look, James," it said.

A slit opened in the wall. It wasn't a window, in fact it was much more like an eyelid, opening upwards. As soon as it started to open the light went out and all the whirrings stopped. The red and gold of sunset shone across the cavern. James crossed the floor and climbed a step to stand beside the Burra and gaze out.

Just outside the window was a tangle of rusty wire, thick enough to screen the slit, so that anyone looking at the cliff would just have seen a mess of wire caught on a ledge half way up. But James could see out quite easily, a bit like hiding in a bush and peering between the leaves. He was about as high above the path as if he'd been looking out of the upstairs window of a house. Beyond the path lay the porridge lake, and the slope he had climbed, and the iron sea, all lit by the fiery sky.

The rats came into sight almost at once. They were as big as Labrador dogs. They wore caps and belts, but no other clothes. Most of them carried their guns slung across their backs and ran on all fours, but some were walking more awkwardly on hind legs, with their guns in their front paws ready and pointing at the sky. James knew which was the officer because it had a sword in its belt and a band of gold round its cap.

The officer squeaked. The patrol halted. More rats rose to their hind legs and aimed their guns at the sky. Five rats from the back of the patrol quickly assembled a small anti-aircraft cannon. As soon as they'd got it loaded and

25

ready the rest of the patrol split up and scurried around, searching the slope. The officer went and inspected the broken trip-wire.

They all moved like ordinary rats, scuttling along with their noses close to the ground and their whiskers quivering. Suddenly one gave an excited squeak and began nosing around the white fridge. Two others joined it and together they came squeaking up towards the cliff.

"I think they've picked up my trail," whispered James.

"Smelt you?" said the Burra, after the usual pause. "We should have thought of that. We do not have any special smell, ourselves. Well, now, let us see . . ."

It did not sound specially worried. In any case James was distracted by a wild squeak from one of the rats by the cannon. All the other rats stopped what they were doing and aimed their guns upward. James heard the whimper of wings and saw the gull for a moment before it soared away out of sight. The rats stayed on the alert for another swoop.

Something nudged against his jeans. He looked down and saw a hairy leg, torn at the top and with sawdust spilling out, nuzzling against him like a too friendly dog. When he tried to back away it followed him.

"Stand still, please," said the Burra. "We must get your smell on us."

James saw that the Burra was standing on its wooden leg now, and it was the camel-leg that had come loose and was doing the nuzzling. He put up with it until the leg seemed to have had enough and went hopping away into the dark.

The rats on the slope below had just relaxed their guard and were starting to search again when there was an explosion of squeaking. Several guns aimed at the cliff, but James couldn't see what the target was until the leg came into sight, darting in zig-zag hops across the slope. The nearest rats rushed at it, trying to catch it, which meant that the others couldn't shoot without hitting them,

26

but as soon as it had dodged clear they started blasting away. They can't have been very good shots, James thought, though the leg was obviously a tricky target, darting about like that. They all missed and the leg could have got clear away, only it suddenly stopped hopping around and stood still on a boulder, outlined against the red sky. It was almost as though it was teasing the rats for their bad shooting.

Several guns banged together. The leg was blasted sideways. Puffs of sawdust shot out and a bit of cloth flapped loose. The leg struggled onto its foot again, although it was cut almost in two half way up. More guns banged and it toppled over, twitched and lay still.

With excited squeaks the rats scuttled towards it, but before they reached it James heard the rush of wings as one of the great gulls came skimming low over the slope from the other side. It almost brushed the backs of the scampering rats as it passed them, scooped the leg into its beak, and slipped away over the ridge and out of sight. The rats only started shooting after it had gone.

The officer was jumping up and down. When it stopped doing that, it rushed at the cannon crew and beat them with the flat of its sword until one of the rats came back from where the leg had fallen carrying something in its mouth. The officer turned with snarling lips, but took the offering, sniffed it and calmed down. It looked like the bit of cloth that had been torn off the leg by the bullets. The officer stuffed it into a pouch and squeaked orders. The patrol packed up its cannon and filed away into the dusk.

James was very glad now that the rats hadn't found him on the slope. Even the idea was frightening, though it hadn't happened. And he felt like crying for the brave leg which had been shot to bits instead of him.

When the slit closed and the light came on he realised something was wrong with the Burra. It was jerking about, and making an extraordinary noise, like a mechanical dog trying to bark.

"Are you all right," said James. "I mean it was awful about your leg."

"We thought it was funny," said the Burra. "Correct us if we are wrong. We have only recently begun to see jokes."

James realised that the noise must be the Burra's idea of laughing.

"It was funny about the officer getting so mad," he said. "But it was sad about your leg."

"We have got plenty more," said the Burra.

"But didn't it hurt?"

"Sawdust does not feel pain."

"Oh. Then it might have been funny. I suppose. The gull nipping in like that, too."

"Good. Now help us across, will you?"

The Burra's furry arm clamped round James's shoulders. With a clump and a clump and a clump, hopping on its wooden leg and resting its weight on James, it crossed to an old tin trunk. On the top, in

28

sloping white letters, was written, "Lieut-Col Aubrey Trout, MC, The Residence, Oodypore". Without the Burra telling it the trunk opened its lid, like a clam in an underwater film. Inside was a mess of coloured legs and arms and heads, which had all once been parts of dolls and cuddly toys. Nine legs wriggled free and lined up in front of the trunk. With James's help the Burra hopped along the line, patting each leg in turn with its green Kermit-hand. Third in line was the pair to the one the Burra was already wearing, but it hopped straight past it.

"Excuse me asking," said James. "Why don't you have that one? I mean, it matches."

The Burra paused even longer than usual.

"Not fair on the rest of us," it said. "Got to keep a balance, especially when it comes to human members. They can be very opinionated, if you don't mind our saying so."

In the end it chose a blue felt leg which might have come off something like a lion. It fitted the leg under its shirt and stood swaying from side to side, adjusting to the new feel.

"Now," it said, "we expect you would like something to eat."

"Yes please," said James.

He was extremely hungry, in spite of having had breakfast not all that long ago. But it was night-time now, and he'd missed his dinner and missed his tea, and he really felt like that. The Burra led the way over to the table, but just as he got there James was struck by an awkward question. What would a creature like the Burra think of as food? Sawdust? Rags?

"If you've got anything," he said.

"If we have got anything!" said the Burra. "We have got everything! People throw everything away, so we have got everything!"

Chapter 5

THE BOX EFFECT

The Burra went into a sort of trance. Its large eye seemed to go dull, but that might have been the loop of light dimming. From the other end of the cavern James heard a rumble, which came nearer and nearer until an old freezer and a gas cooker trundled up to the table. The freezer opened its lid for James to look inside. It was packed with food, icy cold. He chose beefburgers, chips and a packet of strawberry ripple ice-cream for afters. The cooker switched on two burners, two pans flipped into place, and the chips and burgers unwrapped themselves and hopped into the pans, turning over when they were brown on one side. A chair walked up. One of its legs didn't belong so it walked with a limp, but it was perfectly steady when James sat on it. The food hopped on to the plates when it was cooked and the plates skimmed themselves on to the table. The freezer and cooker trundled away, and at the same time the light brightened and the Burra seemed to wake up.

James stared at the good food. His mouth was watering. But . . .

"Is it alive?" he whispered.

"Yes."

"Oh, then I can't . . ."

"It is less alive than it was when it was a cow and a plant. It is less alive than it will be if you eat it. It never chose to become chips and burgers, but since that has happened it would prefer to go through with the job. If you do not eat it it will become rubbish again. We do not like being rubbish. We are trying not to be."

James chose the smallest chip and nibbled the end off. It tasted just ordinary. So did the burgers. He was chewing a proper mouthful when another thought struck him. The way the Burra kept talking about "We".

"Is this food part of you?" he said.

"It was some of us."

"That's not English."

"Then it must be Dumpish. In any case it is now becoming part of you."

"Some of you—inside me?"

"We do not see what you are worrying about. After all, you are inside us at the moment."

"What do you mean?"

The Burra waved its green arm at the walls of the cavern.

"All this is us," it said. "This part here . . ."

It tapped itself on the chest.

". . . this part here is only what you might call a central committee. The Burra Council. Ho ho."

"Oh. Is that why there's a sort of gap before you say anything?"

"We are a democratic institution. We ask around."

"How did you begin, then? I mean, did you have a mum and dad? Or anything?"

"No. Though our first voice came from a doll and said 'Mama' and 'Papa'. It was not much use. This one came from a video game. What do you think of it?"

"Pretty good," said James, mumbling because he'd started eating again without noticing. "Do you mean you just happened?"

"We are not quite sure. But we think we are the result of the Dump ceasing to function."

"What's that mean?"

"We do not know. It is just a feeling we have."

"I still don't understand," said James. "I saw everything outside's sort of gone fossil. And why's it all so enormous? Is that because of the Dump getting stuck? What do you mean, stuck? Like an engine seizing up?"

"A bit like that, we think. We don't really understand ourself. But nothing is totally dead, you know. Everything is a bit alive, only it is a shapeless kind of life. Unorganised. People get hold of that loose life-stuff and give it a bit of shape and use it for a year or two. Then they throw it away. Nature does much the same. It seems a pity, but it is all part of a process—or it was until the Dump ceased to function. Then most of the stuff here did what you call 'going fossil', but some of us somehow put our lives together and started to become what we are now."

"What were you like then?"

"We do not remember. Do you remember when you were a jelly-fish? Ages ago some cells decided to work together and help each other, so they invented themselves into a jelly-fish. That was how you started. If you can, we can too. It is the logical way to go about things."

"But I'm me. You keep talking about 'we' and 'us'."

"You may not be as different as you think. You just feel more like an 'I' inside that skin of yours. We are looser."

Up on the roof the light twisted itself into new coils, as if it was trying to help explain. James remembered how it had dimmed, and how the Burra had gone into a trance while his supper was getting ready. The "life" must have been busy doing the cooking. Now he suddenly felt that the whole cavern, with its faint lights and hums, really was all alive, all one creature, which twitched and quivered the whole time, a bit like a dog having a dream. The Burra didn't even stop where the cavern stopped. It said it had felt him walk into the trip-wire.

The trip-wire reminded him of something else.

33

"What about the rats?" he said. "And the gulls? I mean, they must have been alive already."

"Yes," said the Burra. "But they have changed, too. They have become more organised."

"They've changed all right," said James. "Guns and things. And so big!"

"It is all a matter of life becoming more and more organised. Nothing is totally dead, as I told you."

"Then I've got something that's totally dead," said James. "Look."

He fished the box out of his anorak pocket and passed it across. It felt perfectly ordinary to him, but the moment the Burra's three-fingered hand closed on it an appalling thing happened.

The Burra fell to bits.

It was like an explosion. James only saw the first instant of it before the light went out, but the great glass eye popped off the head and the head jumped away from the shoulders and so did the arms. Then the leg of James's chair which didn't belong came loose and the chair tilted him out on to the floor. By the time he'd scrambled to his feet the bits of the Burra had stopped thumping on to the floor and the cavern was dark.

No, not quite dark. Right up at the far end a few lights blinked off and on. Something up there clunked, whirred and stopped with a louder clunk. It was the noise Mum's old fridge had made when it went wonky. A vacuum-cleaner started and stopped. A bit nearer a TV screen switched itself on for a moment, showing jagged interference patterns.

"Burra," James whispered. "Are you all right, Burra?"

No answer. But James could feel that something was still there. All around him in the darkened cavern something was trying to happen, trying to come to life.

It was the box's fault. The first thing to do was to find the box and put it back in his pocket. He got down on his knees and patted around. Lots of loose things were lying on the floor. The back of his hand brushed something furry and he picked it up. The Burra's teddy-bear arm. It twitched slightly in his grip. That was a good sign. If only he could find the box.

He was groping about under the table when something with a loose, floppy feel brushed the back of his neck. He shrank away, then forced himself to reach up and find what it was. Cloth, with padding inside and some bendy wire. The Kermit arm, dangling over the edge of the table. He rose to his feet and felt along the limp tube. No twitch of life there. But at the far end the three fingers were still clamped round the box.

With a sigh of relief James prized them loose and shoved the box into his pocket. Almost at once several more lights came on at the far end of the cavern, and the wonky-fridge noise steadied to a whirr. The TV set turned itself on and switched through several channels, all showing rats doing things. The table creaked. Slowly, jerkily, the light-tube started to glow.

The Burra—at least the creature that walked and talked, though it said it was only part of the whole Burra—the Burra still lay around in pieces on the floor. The legs and arms twitched. The donkey's mouth opened and closed like a gaping fish. James couldn't stand that, so he picked the body up and shoved it into the chair. It nearly fell out again because of the chair only having three legs, but when James picked up the loose one to prop it steady, the wood suddenly jumped in his hand and clicked into place.

He lifted the head up and tried to fit it into the collar of the sailor shirt. It didn't want to stick—why should it? It was only a loose bit of broken toy, and the body under the sailor-shirt seemed to be just an old duffel-bag full of lumpy bits and pieces.

James was standing there, wondering whether there was any glue in the cavern, or some string perhaps, when the head wriggled. He let go and it stayed in the right place, shaking itself slowly to and fro, like a TV comic who's been bonked on the head. The mouth stopped gaping and the big floppy ears stood straight up.

He went to fetch the teddy-bear arm but while he was getting it the two legs stood up of their own accord and hopped into place. The eye came rolling across the floor and stuck fast as soon as James fitted it to the side of the head. Only the green arm stayed lifeless on the table. It hung limp when James picked it up and showed no sign of wanting to fix on to the shoulder.

"Who are we?" said the Burra suddenly.

"You're the Burra. I'm James."

"How do you do? The Burra, eh? Yes, yes, of course. The Dump Burra. What happened?"

"I showed you my box of nothing and as soon as you touched it you fell apart. And all the lights went out."

"Very alarming. For all of us, including you no doubt."

"I've just thought of something. When I found my box it was touching an old bucket and a fridge. They were real."

"Real?"

"I mean they hadn't gone fossil. Everything else out there had. And when you touched it . . . I think it turns things back into what they used to be. When it touches them, you see. The things up at the other end there didn't go right out. They kept trying to work, because they were further away."

The Burra stayed silent for a long time.

"Yes," it said suddenly. "Some of us up there remember. We were being sucked into blackness and cold, but we managed to cut ourselves off by falling to bits. That was it. How very extraordinary. What an odd world we live in, to be sure."

"You do," said James. "I don't. Anyway, not usually."

The Burra flopped back in its chair and laughed its donkey-laugh till the cavern echoed.

Chapter 6

NO WAY HOME

It took a whole day for the Burra's green arm to come to life again. In the meanwhile it made do with a monkey arm, which wasn't as useful. The table set firm at the same time, and the fridge out on the slope had "gone fossil" a little earlier. By then James was almost used to eating food which cooked itself and watching a TV which switched itself off and on when it felt like it and sleeping in a living bed. The bed was specially good. It snuggled round you when you got into it, and the blankets tucked themselves against your spine to keep the draughts out, and in the morning they folded themselves tidy while you were having breakfast.

But it wasn't the same as James's own bed. It wasn't home. The cavern was interesting for a bit, and a friendly place, and the Burra did its best, but quite soon James was longing for Floral Street and Mum rabbitting on about everything and Angie mooning her way through her own dream world and the twins dribbling and squabbling. Just before bed on his second evening he went to the window and looked out across the iron sea. There were clouds on the far horizon, two large flat ones and a smaller pointy one between. If the flat roofs of the two warehouses and the pointed roof of the Nothing Shop had been clouds, they might have been that shape. Again in the silence of dusk James thought he heard his name being called. No, not heard—felt. The feeling came to him like a radio signal across the iron sea.

He woke up with an idea. He must have had it in his sleep, because it was there, ready, as soon as he opened his eyes. After breakfast he would go back down to the shore and dip his box of nothing into the iron sea. It might work. After all, the box had somehow turned the fridge and the bucket into what they used to be back in James's world (which he couldn't help thinking of as the *real* world, though the Burra's world seemed completely real while you were in it, much realler than any dream). And the box had made the Burra fall back into the pieces it was made of. Perhaps it would turn the sea back into a fence, and he could find the hole and slip through.

"We suppose it's worth a try," said the Burra. "Mark you, it may not work. Don't build too much on it. The sea isn't part of the Dump. It's different."

"What do you mean different?"

"We do not know. Perhaps we'll find out now."

But it was no good that day. There were too many rats about. A patrol turned up soon after breakfast and spent all morning sniffing about on the slope and fixing extra trip-wires and booby traps, and then another one came along in the afternoon and walked straight into one of the booby traps which meant that a lot more rats came bombing out to see what they'd caught and the whole slope swarmed with them, jumping up and down and squeaking at each other. Next day was almost as bad, but on the third morning the TV switched itself on without being asked. James had been surprised to find that the Dump had its own TV, but it turned out to be rat TV, which was worse than nothing. He couldn't understand the squeaky rat language, of course, though the Burra had learnt a bit, but suppose he could he wouldn't have wanted to watch endless lectures about rat economics or endless films about heroic rat workers in factories. This was a bit more interesting. The TV showed an enormous

38

military parade marching past a saluting base.

"It must be General Weil's birthday," said the Burra. "Or something."

"Who's General Weil?"

"The rat president. There won't be any patrols on his birthday—they'll all be too busy marching around. Good day for finding new members."

"What does that mean?"

"You'll see."

The Burra carried James down as far as the bubbling lake, in case he left any human scent too close to the cavern and got the rats interested again. Then James worked his way back down to the shore, scrambling over the fossil rubbish, aiming as near as he could for the place he'd landed. He kept telling himself not to hope for too much, but he couldn't help it. In fact he ran the last bit, leaping from jut to jut, but when he stood panting on the crunching edge where the waves lapped he was afraid to try until the Burra caught up.

"Well," said the Burra. "Any good?"

"I was waiting to say goodbye."

"All right."

James crouched by the sea's edge. The gravelly surface was quite dry. He noticed that where a wave pushed a lacy fringe of water up the shore and then pulled it back the pebbles it left behind didn't glisten the way they ought to. The water left them dry as a bone.

His heart thumped as he dipped the box into the water. He pushed it right under. The brown cardboard shone like silver. His hand and arm tingled strangely, but nothing else happened. The sea was still there, and the long and empty shore.

"The water is not touching it," said the Burra. "Look. That is why it is silver. It is keeping the water away. How odd."

James pulled the box out. It was dry, though his hand was wet. A dribble of water from his skin slid on to the box and immediately turned into little round drops which scuttered about like water dropped on the hot plate of a cooker. James scooped some water up with his other hand and poured it on to the box. It almost exploded away.

"Very odd," said the Burra. "But it does not look as though your idea is going to work."

"No," said James.

"Bad luck. Come and help us look for new members."

This turned out to be beachcombing, really. The Burra wandered along the shore inspecting all the rubbish that had been washed up in the night. It chose some very odd things, a rubber bathmat, the flexible hose of a vacuum cleaner, a pink lampshade, a wellington boot. It picked them up and carried them for a bit and when it put them down they were alive and followed it around flumping or slithering along like ducklings after their mother. James was too depressed to pay much attention. He tried his box out on bits of fossil rubbish to see if it was still working, and it turned them back into what they used to be all right, but when he dipped it in the sea it was still no good. There was always that silvery layer of

air between the cardboard and the water. He was glad when they went back up to the cavern at the end of the morning.

The rat parade hadn't finished. Some strange old First War tanks were grumbling past a saluting base. The rats who were taking the salute wore enormous caps with rows and rows of gold braid round them. The one in the middle, a small grey animal, had twice as much braid as any of the others, and its cap had to be absolutely enormous to take it all. When the tanks had gone this rat started to make a speech.

It squeaked away for a few minutes, quite calmly, but soon its voice got shriller. Its fur bristled. It gave a couple of hops. It banged the rail in front of it with its fist, then raised a quivering arm and pointed at the sky. Whenever it stopped for breath the other rats on the dais clapped and the soldiers and civilians cheered and gave what seemed to be the rat salute, one arm up with the paw clenched. The rat making the speech worked itself into such a frenzy that it almost fell off the platform. It grabbed something from the rat beside it and waved it in the air. The thing looked like an old rag, but all the rats became extremely excited. The civilians screamed and the soldiers loosed off volleys into the air.

"Hello, that looks like a piece of our old leg," said the Burra.

"The one the patrol shot? And the gull nicked?"

"We think so."

"Is that General Weil making the speech?"

"Indeed it is."

The camera lingered on the screaming crowd. It ought to have been funny, seeing all those rats getting worked up about a bit of old camel-leg, but there were so many of them and they seemed so furious it was frightening. At last the camera returned to General Weil.

"Do you think he's mad at the gulls for nicking your old leg," said James.

"We suppose so. We suppose that to run a place like Rat City you need enemies to blame things on."

"How is he going to fight the gulls? Have they got aeroplanes? It's funny how ancient their tanks are, when they've got TV."

"It depends on what comes to the Dump. There are plenty of TV sets but not much in the way of weapons. They have to invent them, but they are quite clever. A little while ago they were still using bows and arrows. We think they will have aeroplanes soon, if they have not got them already."

"It's funny, isn't it? The rats turning into super-rats and the gulls turning into super-gulls? I wonder why."

"It is all because of the Dump ceasing to function."

"You keep saying that. What does it mean?"

"We do not know. It is just a feeling we have. Something has gone wrong. Over there somewhere."

The Burra waved its green arm towards the back of the cavern.

"But it's only a feeling," said James. "You don't *know*."

"When you are ill you do not know what is wrong," said the Burra. "You just feel something is, and you probably feel where. We are part of the Dump. We have its feelings. You might almost say we *are* its feelings. And we feel something is wrong."

Chapter 7

AWKWARD MEMBER

That evening the Burra decided to have what it called "a snooze". This meant it had taken its head off and left it lying on the table, staring at the roof. The arms lay beside it. The green one seemed to be having a dream—at any rate it kept twitching into Muppety shapes. The wooden leg had hopped over to the tin chest to talk to its twin— not really talk, of course, but they seemed to like being together.

James knew how they felt. They were family. His own family was in a different world, and though they often drove him mad when he was with them it was surprising how much he missed them now. To take his mind off that sort of thing he was drawing with some pencils he'd found. It was rather interesting drawing with the Burra's pencils, because they helped and you got much better pictures than usual. Now he'd taken out the messy conker-tree he'd drawn for Mrs Last to see if the pencils could do anything about it, and they really had, only it wasn't a conker tree any more.

It had a tremendous black swirling trunk and at the top the branches came snaking out like trails of fireworks. All along the branches grew the seeds. The seeds were stars. The Burra had picked up some good bright colours on the beach, so the stars blazed and glittered in the dark tornado of the tree-top. It would be much the best picture anybody had done for Mrs Last if he could only get home with it. He would have to think of a seed, of course. A seed for a star-tree.

He was still putting in stars, not really noticing, when he had a new idea about getting home.

"I think we'd better go and find out what's wrong with the Dump," he said.

"Eeaaaay?" said the Burra's head, just like a donkey braying.

"You keep saying the Dump's gone wrong. Let's go and find out why. It's better than staying here."

The Burra's arms picked up the head and placed it on the shoulders. The leg came clumping across and joined the body.

"You do not like it here?" said the Burra.

"I didn't mean that. I like you a lot. But I want to go home."

"Yes, we suppose so," said the Burra.

"I've thought of building a boat, but the wind and the waves would keep pushing it back, so that's no good. The reason why everything here is the way it is is because the Dump's gone wrong, right?"

"We think so."

"So if we found out why it had gone wrong we might be able to put it right and then that beastly sea would turn back into a fence and I could go home."

"Difficult," said the Burra.

"You don't know till you've tried."

"That is the difficulty. We suppose you cannot help thinking that this bit here . . ." (the green arm tapped the sailor suit) ". . . this bit here is *us*, but it is not. It is only some of us."

"You mean you've all got to go? Cookers and everything?"

"Well, not *all*. No. Not really *all*. But quite a lot of us, to be any good."

"Oh."

44

"We have to admit we have been thinking about this before you came. We have had a vague feeling we ought to be doing something."

"Can't you think of a way? You're terribly clever."

"Not clever enough. If only. . . . Ah well."

"What's the matter?"

The Burra stood up. It seemed gloomy and unwilling, but it led the way up the cavern to the end where most of the stores were. An old wooden box stood against the wall. Usually boxes and things opened themselves when the Burra approached, but this time it lifted the lid itself and peered doubtfully in, with its head cocked to one side.

James looked, expecting to see something dreadful, but it was only the control box of a home computer which somebody must have thrown out. You could see why, too. All over the keyboard and down one side yucky pink paint had been spilt, the colour of the sort of ice-cream that is pretending to be made of raspberries when it's really come out of a chemistry factory.

"Does it work?" said James. "Terry at school's dad's got one like that."

The Burra didn't answer, but continued to stare gloomily into the box.

"You really think we ought to go and find out what is wrong with the Dump?" it said at last.

"I don't know about ought. I just want to. In fact I've got to. If you don't want to come I'll have to go by myself. If I can."

"You see," said the Burra, "we think this will be a very difficult member. When we first asked it to join it was not at all co-operative. Very withdrawn and ill-tempered. We need a member like this if we are going to move around, but . . . ah well . . . we suppose we will have to give it a try. Be kind enough to carry it over to the table for us, will you?"

Under the loop of light the paint-splash looked even

45

yuckier. The Burra put out its green arm and then pulled it back.

"You know," it said, "even our pocket calculator tried to boss us around when it first joined us. That is no good. We have to keep a balance. That is why we chose this head—it does not get ideas above itself."

The worn old ears twitched, like a dog's do when it knows it's being talked about. The whole cavern seemed to go still. The Burra laid its green fingertips gently on the computer casing. Nothing happened.

"Very withdrawn," said the Burra. "Perhaps we had better . . ."

There was a click. The "On" light glowed. The Burra's ears stood bolt upright as if it was having an electric shock. The TV switched itself on and started playing a video game at twenty times the proper speed. The Burra's jaw gaped and its voice came out as a high twitter, like a tape being rapid-wound.

This lasted just a few seconds. Then it all got worse. The TV screen was covered with jagged bright shapes, and its sound-track came on full volume, all bangs and crashes and screechings. The Burra's arms and legs jerked around like one of the twins in a tantrum, but far worse, so that James could see it was going to flog itself to bits. He had to do something to stop it, but the moment he tried to reach out and grab the green arm off the computer, something hit him. Not in one place, all over, like a ball being hit by a tennis racket.

The blow slung him across the cavern and sprawled him on to his bed. As soon as he touched it the mattress rose up at each end and gripped him. He kicked and wriggled, but the blankets coiled themselves round his legs and tightened fast. The noise in the cavern was deafening, not just the TV, but everything else rumbling around, clattering and whirring, and the Burra's high agonising twitter on top of it all. The tube light flickered

on and off, sometimes too bright to look at, so that the wriggling shape stayed glaring on James's eyeballs through the next patch of dark.

His arm was pinned across his body so tight that it hurt, but when he tried to ease it the mattress squeezed tighter. The movement pushed his hand against something hard. His box of nothing in the pocket of his anorak, which he'd left lying on the bed. Now he could just slither his fingertips into the pocket and coax the box out. The mattress seemed to notice the movement and squeezed tighter, but it was too late. James shoved a corner of the box against it. At the first touch it flopped loose. He prodded the box against the blankets and they fell away. He stood up.

The light came coiling down at him from the ceiling like a fiery snake. All the stuff in the cavern rushed towards him, but it wasn't quick enough. He ran to the table, holding the box in front of him. The light darkened and arched out of his way. He banged the box hard down on the "Off" key of the computer.

Silence. The TV switched off. The light-tube dimmed to orange and dragged itself back to the ceiling. The Burra gave a violent shudder, gripped the edge of the table and stood swaying and shaking its head.

"We think we had better have a little rest," it said, and flopped into the chair. Slowly the rest of the stuff in the cavern rumbled back to its places. The light grew brighter. The Burra twitched and muttered.

"Are you all right?" said James.

"A very unpleasant experience," said the Burra.

"Everything seemed to go mad," said James. "My bed joined in."

"Mad? Deranged, certainly."

"But you're better now."

"Yes, thank you. The problem, you see, is this. Most of our new members have something wrong with them when they join. That is why people threw them away in the first place. We can help them to mend themselves, but only if they co-operate. We do not see how we can begin to co-operate with a member who insists on taking complete control of the rest of us."

James stared at the computer. The paint was a specially nasty colour, he thought, and a specially nasty shape too.

"I expect I'd go a bit mad if I'd got something yuck like that dribbling around in my brain," he said.

The Burra cocked its head on one side and stared at the computer.

"You may be right," it said. "Perhaps it is worth another try. Stand by with that box of yours."

James held the box close above the "Off" key while the Burra reached out with one green finger and gently touched the paint. Nothing happened.

"Best we can do," said the Burra. "You cannot expect quick responses from spilt paint. Very low degree of organisation there."

The Burra was still wary of touching the computer, so James carried it back up the cavern and put it in its chest. Before he went to bed he had a look and saw that the paint seemed to have gone soft and was gathering into a blob. Some of it was dribbling down the side of the casing.

Next morning, first thing, he went to look again. The Burra didn't seem to be around, but the chest opened itself as James approached. The computer had switched itself on and was humming quietly. All the paint had flowed off the top and down the side, where it had set into a fat, pink, heart-shaped bulge, just like the heart on the greeting card James had bought for Gran's last birthday.

Chapter 8

GOING EXPLORING

Things started happening while James was still having his breakfast. Piles of copper pipes and nylon curtain rails and lengths of old electric cable unstacked themselves and began a sort of dance on a clear bit of floor, weaving in and out of each other incredibly fast. It reminded James of something. He couldn't think what for a moment, then he realised it was a bit like Mum knitting. If you could imagine a giant bit of knitting going on, only the giant and the knitting-needles were invisible, and the knitting process was happening in several places at once. Soon James could see a shape beginning to grow, a long, narrow, canoe-shaped giant sort of basket.

Just beyond that something different was happening. He took his Rice Krispies up there so that he could watch. Half a dozen old lawn mowers had trundled together into a group and were taking themselves to bits, groaning and creaking a bit, like old gentlemen complaining about their hips. A couple of oil cans hopped among them, easing the rusty nuts, like metal humming-birds. The bits began to build themselves into a new engine.

Next door to that a jumble of electrical oddments was sorting itself into what seemed to be three separate gadgets which James didn't undertstand at all. A soldering iron strutted among the web of wires. As soon as they were joined up they coiled themselves away into three blue milk-crates. Close by, two large saucepan lids were gently easing themselves into dish shapes.

The funny thing was that all this was going on while the walking-talking part of the Burra wasn't there. Usually when that happened the cavern went almost to sleep, but now it was busier than James had ever seen it. Suddenly he had a thought. Perhaps the computer *had* taken over. It had got rid of James's friend in the night, taken it to bits, thrown it out, forced it to become just rubbish again.

Trying not to show he was worried James strolled across to the window. The slit opened for him in the usual friendly way, and he gazed out. Something extraordinary was happening down on the shore, a sort of bright-coloured whirlwind moving along close to the sea's edge. At the foot of it walked the familiar shape of the Burra. It was collecting plastic bags. Thousands of them, and more and more flapping up to join the funnel-shaped whirling column that followed the Burra along the line of rubbish. If a rat patrol came along now, James thought, it would have something to shoot at.

Not just the whirlwind, either. Something was happening down by the porridge lake, but he couldn't see what. Some sort of engine was pumping away, and a lot of tubes were wandering around on top of the surface. Wherever a hummock grew they darted over and sucked the gas in. It was fascinating to watch, a bit like a video game.

The Burra was coming back up the slope now, with its whirlwind still following it. A huge ball came bouncing up beside it. As soon as they all reached the slope below the cliff the whirlwind flopped down and the thousands of plastic bags flummocked around sorting themselves into sizes. The ball turned out to be an enormous roll of coarse cord.

The Burra itself came in and laid a friendly green hand

on the computer, which answered with a lot of quick bips, almost like a song.

"Is it all right now?" said James.

"Fully recovered and eager to join in."

"That's brilliant. What are you going to do if a rat patrol comes along?"

"There will be time to hide. We have put sensors out. The computer has greatly extended our range for that sort of thing."

"What's happening?"

"Ho ho."

"Oh, come on!"

"We want it to be a surprise. Ho ho."

All afternoon the cavern got busier and busier. The bustle was still going on when James went to bed. He found it difficult to sleep. He kept half waking, half opening his eyes, half seeing something new being done, half dreaming he'd seen it, and by that time he was half asleep again. For instance, he saw, or dreamed, that the plastic bags were slithering around the floor, melting into each other and making an enormous patchwork sheet, which rolled itself up at one end as it was joined together. Later he dreamed that Mum was pushing the twin's pram across the floor of the cavern, then woke enough to see that the basket-thing had finished knitting itself and had been joined by two sets of pram wheels which it was trying out. One of them twittered, just like the twins'.

The engine started up. It made an incredible racket and a foul smell, far worse than petrol. Whatever it was using must be made from the gas in the porridge lake, somehow. Luckily it only ran for a minute, then trundled itself over to the basket-thing, which tipped sideways to help it climb in. The whole contraption wheeled away and squeezed itself out down the stairs.

Next time James woke he saw the huge ball of string rolling to and fro across the floor knotting itself into a kind of net, a bit like the string bag Gran used for groceries, only big enough to hold twenty elephants. James watched for a bit and fell asleep again. Next thing he knew, his mattress had tipped him out on to the floor. It had done it on purpose. The Burra was standing there looking down at him.

"Ho ho," it said.

"Very funny," said James. "What's the big idea? Where's everything, anyway?"

The cavern had gone very quiet, and all the things that had been clattering around before had disappeared.

"The sensors report movement up the mountain. We think the rats have sent out a night patrol."

"They must have spotted something going on this afternoon."

"Probably. But we are ready to go, in any case."

Shivering, James dressed. His clothes weren't part of the Burra so they didn't do things for themselves. As soon as he'd got his anorak on one of his blankets wriggled up and wrapped itself round his shoulders like a cloak. He patted his mattress goodbye and followed the Burra to the stairs. The cavern seemed to have gone fast asleep, as though almost all the "life" that had kept it humming and twitching had left.

He was glad of the blanket when they got outside. It was bitter cold, with a black sky full of sharp little stars. Down by the porridge lake he could hear a pump still chugging, but everything else seemed still. The Burra took his elbow to guide him down the path. When they got to the trip-wire a faint light shone so that he could see to step over it. Now he could hear the plop and suck of bubbles rising in the lake and smell the stinking gas.

At the lake's edge the light shone again, just enough for James to see the edge of the basket-thing.

"In we get," said the Burra.

James climbed over and picked his way through a jumble of things from the cavern to a clear space. The

basket creaked at every step, and something else answered with fainter creaks above him. When he had settled he looked up, but could see nothing but blackness. No stars, even. Something huge was blotting out the sky, stirring a little as the breeze off the sea shifted it to and fro, and creaking as the immense net of knots and cords that held it in place took the strain.

The pump stopped. With a series of plops the tubes fell clear. Rustling whispers began as ropes untied themselves all round. In a sudden patch of quiet James heard scurryings from up the path, the clink of metal on rock, a squeak of challenge.

The last ropes fell free, timing it almost perfectly, so that the basket scarcely swayed as the Burra's home-made airship floated silently up through the night.

Chapter 9

OVER THE MOUNTAINS

The wind blew steadily from the sea, pushing the airship inland. James could see the peaks ahead by the jagged line where the stars ended and there was only blackness below them.

It became colder as the airship rose. He shivered, and immediately another blanket came slithering along and wrapped itself round him. When he moved, the basket-work beneath him changed shape to make him comfort-able. He had been wrong about the airship being home-made, he realised. It was home-grown, more like. It was all alive, the way the cavern had been alive. Some-how the Burra had managed to become an airship, in order to go exploring.

"When are you going to start your engine?" he said.

"Not until we have to."

"What does it run on?"

"Fractionated by-products formed in the extraction of hydrogen from sewage-gas."

"How did you know how?"

"We thought it up with our computer."

"That's brilliant. Have you brought the computer with you?"

"Of course. The whole trip would be impossible with-out it."

"What will happen when the gulls see us?"

"It will be all right."

As the airship climbed the mountains climbed too. It was difficult to see with everything so black, but sometimes James felt that the harsh slope was only just below them, although a moment before they had seemed to be floating miles above it. There was almost no wind. Or rather the airship was moving with the wind, so though it might be rushing along the air around it seemed still.

Suddenly, almost straight ahead, James saw the glitter of starlit snow.

"Look out!" he yelled.

The noisy motor started before the shout was over. A propeller whupped at air. Slowly the ship swung sideways, almost grazing the cliff. The basket rocked violently where the wind buffeted into the mountain. The ship swung on until the nose pointed into the wind. Now every rope and cord shrieked in the streaming air as the engine slowly threshed their way out of danger.

As soon as they were clear it slowed, working only hard enough to keep them over the same spot as they floated up and up until they were above the level of the peaks. Then the ship turned, the engine cut out, the shrieking of the cords died away and they swept silently on above the jagged ridges.

From this height James could see, far to the right, a faint paling of the sky and a silvery pink line along the sea, ending where the mountains broke the horizon. The range seemed to go on for ever. He remembered the Dump he used to know, the one you saw across the road when you turned out of Floral Street. You could bike round that and be back in ten minutes, easy.

"Why's it all got so big?" he said.

"We don't know but we hope to find out. Now, look there!"

James twisted to crane over the other side of the basket. He gasped. They had crossed the mountain wall and reached a large inland plain. It ought still to have been

56

pitch dark down there, out of reach of the first dawn light, but it wasn't.

Pale street lighting threaded its way in criss-cross patterns, dotted lines of lamps running endlessly across the plain, as far as he could see. In some places there were fuzzy patches, vaguely lit with orange, where trails of smoke blotted out the street-lamps. Separate from these James saw two squares of much brighter light.

The first was just a very big flood-lit building, some kind of Town Hall by the look of it. The other one was different, because the square of brightness ran round a darker patch in the centre, but there was still enough light there for James to see rows and rows of huts. A line of guard towers stood in the bright-lit border of the square, but it was too far away for him to see the fence between them. He knew it must be there, from films he'd seen at home on TV.

"It seems they still use gas lighting for most things," said the Burra. "Electricity is for what they consider important. That must be General Weil's palace."

"And his prison camp, I suppose," said James. "He's that sort. What's the orange bits?"

"Furnaces. Iron foundries. There is a lot of iron to be mined out of the Dump."

Slowly the sky turned paler, and as it did so the lights below grew faint and went out. Soon James could see the endless lines of little houses, street after street of them, cramped and huddled. They weren't even proper houses —sheds and huts, some round like mud huts in safari films, some patched out of corrugated iron and other rubbish. But all so crammed, and not a garden anywhere. The streets ran every which way, except in a few places where a grand highway had been carved through the muddle, or where railway-lines snaked their way into the city, with early trains puffing along under trails of greasy smoke. The first rat workers, tiny dots from this height, were scurrying through the dawn streets. James didn't

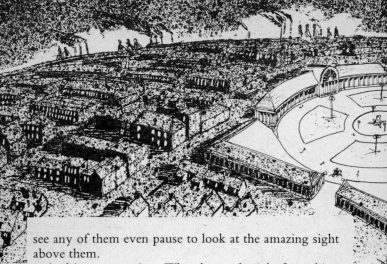

see any of them even pause to look at the amazing sight above them.

And it was amazing. When he got bored of watching the huge grey slum below—depressing and also a bit frightening—he turned his attention to the airship. This was more fun.

The plastic bags which the Burra had collected on the shore had melted themselves into a single enormous bag, a patchwork of different colours, the blue sort which farmers buy fertiliser in and green Marks and Spencer shopping bags, and pink and mauve ones from posh dress shops, and yellow ones from places like DIY shops and drinks stores, all jumbled together without any pattern, just lovely splodges of colour compared with the drab grey city below. The plastic must be several layers thick, for strength, James thought, and the whole bag was held into shape by the great upside-down string net-bag which he'd seen weaving itself on the cavern floor. Extra strong cords ran down from this to carry the basket in which he sat.

It was more like a canoe than a basket, really, except for having wheels and being full of holes. It was tiny compared with the gas-bag, but it was crammed with

oddments from the cavern. They weren't the sort of
thing you'd take on an expedition either. There was a
dressmaker's dummy and a stuffed fish and the light-coil
and an old wind-up gramophone with a horn and an
ironing board and a supermarket trolley and a lot of other
junk. He remembered some of it from the cavern, though
it had never done anything there. He was staring at the
stuffed fish when it winked at him. Of course it was alive,
and so were all the other things. They were all members
of the Burra—the Burra Council, elected to come on this
expedition. The Burra had explained about that, hadn't
it?

And the bits of the airship must be members too, the basket and the engine and even the ropes and plastic bags. The computer, of course, and the electrical gadgets James had seen making themselves in the cavern. Two of these, in their milk crates, sat in the prow and stern with their re-shaped saucepan lids on top. Some kind of radar, James thought. The third one was under the computer, near the middle.

"Do we just go where the wind pushes us?" James asked.

"We can go where we like if we use our engine," said the Burra. "But fuel is limited and we may need most of it to come back. For the moment the wind is taking us the way we feel is right. We can make minor adjustments with some fins we have, like a fish's, on top of the gas-bag."

"That's brilliant too."

"Thank you. We are quite pleased with ourselves so far."

"It's terrific to be going somewhere. I like you, Burra, but I do want to go home. I don't really belong here, you see. Do you think we're really going to be able to do something about the Dump? Just us, when there's such a lot of it?"

The Burra was silent for quite a long time.

"We think there must be a reason for things," it said at last. "We may look like a complete accident, but we do not feel like one. We do not feel that you are here by accident, James, with your box. So perhaps we are doing the right thing. Now you will have to stop talking while we see how effective our next contraption turns out."

"What do you mean?"

"Look over there. The gulls are coming."

Chapter 10

GULL ATTACK

By now the sun was over the mountains, though the great Rat City still lay in shadow below. The snow peaks glittered in the sideways light. Looking along the line of the Burra's arm James saw several flecks of pure white floating in the brilliant air. He counted nine. Gulls.

He remembered gulls at the seaside, the fierce ripping beaks, the way they snatched a thrown crust out of the air, their small eyes, yellow and cruel. These gulls were a hundred times that size, and the gas-bag that carried him and the Burra was soft, so easy a target. In spite of what the Burra had said, James was scared.

"What will they do?" he said.

"Please do not talk," said the Burra. "We need to concentrate. But it will be all right."

It took a spare eye out of its shirt pocket and screwed it into the back of its head, between the ears, then settled by the computer. The milk crate under the computer began to hum. So did the two at the front and back of the basket. The saucepan lids stood up on extending stalks so that they looked like metal flowers. Surprisingly the engine didn't start up, but James could feel that the whole airship had changed slightly, had come fully awake, tense and ready.

And only just in time.

The gulls came incredibly fast. A few seconds ago

they'd been white specks in the blue morning sky, but now they were birds, skimming in perfect formation towards the airship. Yes, nine of them. They grew and grew. The Burra didn't seem to be doing anything.

They looked as if they meant to ram straight into the gas-bag, but when they were about a hundred yards away James heard a single harsh squawk and they peeled off to the left in perfect formation, like the Red Arrows doing a display. They circled the airship twice in silence, apart from the hiss of wind over their feathers. Another squawk, and the flanker broke formation and headed in. Straight for the basket. Straight at James.

He stared, frozen, at the great yellow beak as it rushed towards him.

The gull fell out of the sky.

It stopped flying. All its feathers stood on end. Its wings went out of control. Its eyes closed. It dropped.

The speed of its flight made it fall in a curve, under the basket and out on the far side. James craned over the edge to watch it tumble. Sad, all that brightness and speed, gone. Dead.

But half way to the ground the gull came alive again. The wings gave a few wild flips, the feathers shook themselves into place and it was a bird, and flying.

It was obviously dazed, and just zig-zagged about until two of its comrades who had gone swooping down to help when it fell joined it and led it back up. The other six, meanwhile, continued to circle the airship.

When they were all nine together again there was a lot of squawking. Then the squadron broke up into three sets of three, flying line ahead round the gas-bag, like Redskins round a wagon camp. This time the attack came without any signal. All at once, all together, three birds swooped in from different directions.

A moment later all three were tumbling out of the sky.

James was watching the one straight in front of him, but he could hear the others hit the invisible barrier, a sort of soft whup, and the rush of flight ending. He looked down to follow their fall. They didn't all three come alive at quite the same time—hitting the barrier seemed to stun some worse than others—but none of them reached the ground, and before long the airship was drifting on with its escort of nine gulls circling well clear of the barrier, puzzled and careful, but not giving up. By no means.

They tried everything. Attacks from below and above. Attacks in mass formation. Attacks in quick succession. Gentle probings and high-speed dives. They were brave all right, because the same thing happened every time—about thirty yards from the airship they met the forcefield and fell. Even accidentally touching it with a wing-tip seemed to do the trick.

James remembered how, when the Burra had first tried to make contact with the computer and it had gone haywire, he'd run in to rescue the Burra and the computer

63

had knocked him right across the cavern. If it could do that when it was mad with pink paint dribbling over its insides, it could easily deal with nine gulls when it was working properly. He began to feel a bit sorry for the gulls.

At first, after he'd got over his fright, James thought it was funny to see those fierce and haughty creatures, white wind-riders, lords of the realm of air, suddenly change to clowns when the currents of the forcefield stood their feathers on end. But as the morning went on he began to think he'd seen the joke often enough.

By now the airship had reached the edge of Rat City, a shambling vague line between sheds and huts on one side and an untidy hummocky empty plain beyond. In one or two places out in this desert there were groups of proper houses, with swimming pools and tennis courts. In a lonely valley there was a huge prison camp near the entrance to a mine. He didn't see a tree or a bush any-where. Some of the rats below seemed to notice what was going on in the sky. Particularly at the prison camp they got highly excited, and a whole regiment of guards rushed out of barracks and took up defensive positions.

At last the gulls seemed to give up, and simply circled gravely around.

"If only we could send a message," said James.

"What sort of a message?" said the Burra. "We do not speak gull. We doubt if we can even think gull."

"I don't know. A sign or something. If I was a gull. . . . You haven't got a white feather anywhere?"

"We could make one," said the Burra.

"A good big one, so we could wave it at them. Only it would be better if we could send it. Sort of more friendly."

"All right," said the Burra.

At James's feet a big white plastic bag—one of the spares the Burra had brought to mend itself with—started to rustle and crinkle. A mid-rib ridged up and a shape

64

grew round it until the bag became a white feather from a gigantic plastic bird. A cord unravelled itself from the net, dangled down and knotted itself round the quill. At the other end of the cord a blister bulged out of the gas-bag, squeezed through the net and became a separate balloon, which drifted gently away from the airship carrying the feather below it. The gulls came closer to watch, but were still careful to keep outside the forcefield. The balloon moved out in a series of jerks, as if it was being patted along by an invisible hand. The gulls drifted by, each with its head cocked to one side as it eyed the Burra's gift. You can't tell what gulls are thinking, James decided. They're too different.

He knew when the balloon reached the barrier because the invisible hand gave it one last extra-strong pat and then it was drifting free, moved only by the wind. A gull came cautiously in and took the cord in its beak. There was a short gull-conference, and then seven of them were soaring away towards a distant line of blue hills at the far edge of the plain. The one with the balloon looked like a child going home from a party. Two stayed to circle the airship, as a guard, or escort.

"Gone to report," said the Burra.

Chapter 11

SECRET WEAPON

Half an hour later James was kneeling with his elbows on the edge of the basket, watching the two gulls circle past. It was not very interesting. There isn't much to do on an airship. Though the Burra had relaxed a bit once it had decided the gulls weren't going to try any more attacks, it was still too busy being an airship to have anything left to amuse James with. So he counted the times the gulls went by.

He made a sort of game of it. There was one bit of the circle where they flew directly in front of the sun. It was too bright for him to watch them pass, so he shut his eyes and swung his head and tried to be looking exactly at the gull when it came out beyond the brightness and he could open his eyes again.

A hundred and one. A hundred and two. A hundred and three. When he reached two hundred he'd think of another game. A hundred and . . .

And the gull wasn't there. Yes it was. It was plummeting down, not flying. Loose feathers drifted above it. There was blood on one wing. The engine had started. No it hadn't. Yes, it had now, but before that there'd been something like another engine, a sort of steady clatter. The other gull was hurtling round from the side. At the edge of the patch of glare where James couldn't look, a dark shape, black against the brightness, grew out of nothing. Its shadow swept across the gas-bag and then it was out of the glare and he could see it, a two-seater biplane, swinging to meet the gull's attack. The gull was far faster, far more at home in the air, but the biplane had guns. James could hear their tokka-tokka above the airship's engine and the biplane's own engine roaring at full throttle. It must have come gliding out of the sun, silent as a bird, and caught the gulls by surprise. It had got one. Now it was battling with the second.

The fight didn't last long. A puff of feathers shot from the gull's wing. The bird jerked in mid-air, gave a violent clumsy flap and rose out of the line of fire of the biplane's fixed front guns, though the rear gunner was still blasting away. The gull struggled clear, flying limpingly with one wing. Against the clear blue sky James could see a whole section of flight-feathers had been shot clean away.

The biplane didn't try to follow it. Instead, while the rear gunner kept the gull at a distance, it turned slowly round and started in towards the airship. James could see it clearly now, just like a World War One fighter, with a radial engine and wings strutted and stayed. The propeller was a circular blur, behind which rose three bumps. The middle one was the head of the rat pilot in helmet and goggles, and the two smaller ones were the synchronised machine-guns on the engine cowl.

Bright orange blobs winked at the muzzles of the guns. And the forcefield didn't work against bullets.

James heard the whum whum whum as they slogged into the gas-bag. For a long, cool moment before things started to happen he had time to think about it. Perhaps the bullets were too small, or they came too fast, or they weren't properly alive, or something. Anyway the Burra hadn't known there'd be a rat aeroplane, and the Burra knew a lot about the rats because the TV told it, even when it wasn't switched on. The biplane must be a state secret. General Weil's secret weapon. That was why he'd got in such a rage against the gulls in the speech James

had watched. He was getting his rats ready to declare war on them. Typical . . .

And then James was gulping with fright. He could hear the gas whistling out of fifty holes. He clutched his blanket round him and felt, somehow, that it was frightened too. It'll be all right, he tried to think. When the biplane reaches the forcefield . . .

But it didn't. Perhaps the pilot had heard what had happened to the gulls. Rats down below must have seen them falling out of the air. Perhaps he didn't want to get too close in case the bag exploded. At any rate, when he was still well clear, he roared his engine and zoomed overhead, out of sight behind the bag and then circling round, turning, slowly, slowly, pointing straight at the airship, coming in again . . .

The hissing had stopped, so the gas-bag must have mended itself. But the engine had stopped too. James noticed that his blanket seemed to have gone dead. Apart from the drone of the approaching engine everything was very still, so still that James noticed the dish of the gadget beside him swivelling round to point at the biplane. The other one was doing the same. They were the only things moving.

Perhaps the Burra would do something this time. Perhaps the computer had thought of a way. It better had.

The orange blobs began again. The bullets whupped in. The pilot wasn't shooting at the gas-bag this time, but

at the basket. Nothing you could do, except sit there waiting to be hit. No use cowering behind the side of the basket. That wouldn't stop a bullet. Better to watch.

Something jarred his right hand, making the whole arm tingle. He thought a bullet had hit him, only there was no blood. Then he saw it was the rope he'd been clutching which had been hit. He'd been gripping it so tight that the blow had travelled right up his arm, as though he was part of the airship too.

The rope wasn't quite cut through. Snaky worms of cord were unwinding themselves round the few tense threads that still joined the two halves and held the basket to the gas-bag. That was all right. The Burra would make them wind up in a second. Only they didn't.

Burning! They were on fire! A foul hot smell like a plastic cup put down on a hot cooker. It was the blue milk crate under the computer beginning to melt. Some of the wires inside it were red hot.

There was a violent, tearing bang. Shafts of blue light, too bright to look at, beamed from the aerials at the ends of the basket. The aerials melted with their heat as they shot through. The bolts of energy came and went so fast that James hadn't time to blink before they were gone. They met and crossed right where the biplane was storming in. The biplane exploded. Wings, tail, engine, fuselage, pilot, gunner went tumbling through the sky in all directions. Done it!

The Burra must have put everything into those twin bolts of energy. Not just what it had to spare—everything it had got. The force had been terrific. It was all over in a second, but as the beams blasted out they made the flimsy basket kick the other way, as if it had been buffeted by a solid lump of air. It swung up and sideways, tried to flip right over, slapped into the gas-bag which stopped it, slumped back on to its ropes. The sudden strain was

too much for those last few threads of the one James had
been holding. They snapped. The basket tilted again,
downwards this time. Somehow the Burra managed to
use its last few scraps of energy to keep itself together
and prevent any of its parts falling out, but James wasn't
one of them.

Desperately he scrabbled for a hold as the basket tipped
further, spilling him right out. The rope was wrenched
from his grasp and he was falling head over heels through
the air.

Chapter 12

CAPTURED

Falling, falling. Air rushing faster and faster. Head over heels. Sky and land whirling upside down. Great white cloud coming. Whump!

Whump into soft white cloud, only it wasn't a cloud, more like some kind of bulgy bed, or a soft white trampoline that has somehow got stuck at the bottom of your jump and won't push you back. Still falling, but not so fast. Sky steady overhead.

Very carefully, because the cloud-thing was wobbly and he was scared of toppling off it, James sat up and looked round. Not far off and a bit above him he saw a rat dangling under an enormous parachute. Even then it took him time to understand that he had fallen on top of the other parachute—there'd been two rats in the biplane, pilot and gunner. This one was falling faster because of James's extra weight. The white cloth bulged up round him so that he couldn't see the ground.

They'd fallen a long way already. High overhead a white gull with a tattered wing was trying to tow the airship away. It had the broken rope in its beak. The gas-bag looked floppy. The basket still dangled sideways and James could just see the Burra lolling limp by the engine. It must still be in some sort of a daze after the fight. Perhaps it would wake up and mend itself and come and rescue him.

He wasn't ready for the landing. He heard a bump below. The bulge of the parachute went out of shape, began to flop, stopped holding him, sent him slithering down, clutching at nothing . . . thump.

A wild squeak. Another thump. He'd landed.

Wasn't hurt, either, only thumped. Fallen on something. The parachute was still flopping softly down as James stood up. A rat with the parachute harness attached was lying on the ground with its eyes open. Dead?

No—it's whiskers were quivering. He must have fallen on top of it and stunned it—yes, thump, squeak, thump, like that. The other parachute was still in the sky. First thing was to get away from the rats and hide somewhere until the Burra came and rescued him. No trees, no bushes, just the bare slopes of a small valley. Get up over the ridge for a start.

He scrambled up the slope, noticing as he did so that it was a bit different from the slope he'd climbed by the iron sea. Not so steep, but that wasn't it. No, it was made of different things. Not cookers and fridges but bits of old wagons, and ploughs, and things like that, all gone fossil. He understood without thinking about it that this was an older kind of place.

He ducked over the ridge, panting, and began to leap from jut to jut down the far slope, watching all the time for his next foot-hold, so that it was not until he reached the bottom of the valley and took a quick look round for a hiding-place that he saw the gull.

It lay on its side near a small black stream. The white

feathers were striped with blood. He thought it was dead, but then it moved a great yellow foot.

He ran over and gazed down. It was big enough to help him fight the second rat if it wasn't too wounded, but when he got near he saw it was really dying. He stood and gazed down at it and the yellow unreadable eye stared back. If only he could do something.

Mop up the blood? No use. Get it a drink of the foul black water? Nothing to carry it in. Better leave it and find somewhere. . . . Perhaps the rat would forget about him once it had found the gull . . .

James had actually turned away when he remembered his box of nothing. It probably wouldn't do any good, but it had helped when the computer had gone mad. And it couldn't do any harm, not if the gull was dying.

He pulled it out of his inside pocket and placed it against the largest patch of blood. His idea, if you could call it that, was that it might somehow unbullet the bullet inside the wound.

The gull stirred at the touch. Then, quick as a blink, it shrank. One moment there'd been a huge, wounded bird lying on its side, and the next there was an ordinary seaside gull struggling to its feet. It strutted a couple of steps and rattled its feathers into place, sending a spatter of little bright things onto the ground. Then it gave James a gull's typical haughty one-eyed stare, stretched its wings and flew off.

James put the box back into his pocket as he watched it go, then picked up one of the bright things that had fallen out of its feathers. It was a scrap of silver paper . . . a sweet-wrapping or something . . . roughly twisted into the shape of a bullet. He was still looking at it and wondering when something squeaked sharply behind him.

He turned. A rat airman was standing there, only a few feet away. It was pointing a huge revolver straight at James's head.

A bit later James was walking along a narrow track, with
the rat he had stunned in front of him and the other rat,
the one with the revolver, behind. Far away to his right
he could see the airship, like a coloured speck in the sky,
being towed by several gulls. It was too small for him to
see whether the Burra had mended itself and got the
basket straight, but anyway none of the gulls had come
to look for him, or for their fallen comrade.

The rats marched on all fours. The one behind carried
the revolver, cocked, in its teeth. Before they'd started,
it had shown James how quickly it could get into the
firing position. Still James kept thinking that he ought to
be able to escape by using his box, somehow getting close
enough to touch a rat and turn it back into an ordinary
animal. If only there weren't two of them. But the one
in front had a revolver in its belt and it would have time
to draw and fire while James was dealing with the one

behind. And anyway, he couldn't be sure whether the box would work on rats. It had on the gull, but then the gull had been dying. Suppose a rat shot at him while he was carrying the box, would the bullet turn into a bit of silver paper before it had hit him? Or after? If only he could be sure how the box worked.

He was still trying to nerve himself to do something when they met the patrol. Or perhaps it was a search party, because four of them were carrying stretchers. The rest were rat soldiers. They all became very excited when they met. The rat officer rubbed whiskers with the pilot and gunner and then the whole lot gathered in a chattering ring round James. The officer pranced up and squeaked at him. James shook his head. The officer pulled out a pistol and began to jump up and down, which seemed to be the rats' habit when they were angry. James became frightened, but at last the officer must have grasped that he couldn't understand rat language. It stopped jumping around and squeaked orders to the others. They all marched down the track.

By the time they reached the railway line James was extremely tired. The rats let him sit down while they got a meal ready. It was just water with a soapy taste and a grey dry mess, like porridge before it's cooked. James found he could eat it by mixing some water with it, but it was too nasty for more than a few mouthfuls. The sun was almost overhead by now. Except for the two who were guarding James, the rats lay around panting in the desert heat.

At last from far across the plain a faint hoot came floating. Everyone jumped up and stared along the dead straight line of the tracks. James could see nothing at first, then there was a blob of smoke, then a dot below the blob, and now a louder hoot and the waff waff waff of the pounding engine. The officer pulled out a huge pistol and fired it into the air. The Verey cartridge soared up and burst into pink light which drifted slowly down. The engine hooted in answer. Its wheels screeched on the track and it came to a halt close by where they were waiting. It was a great black beast of a machine, far more impressive than the gibbering rats, but its driver was a rat too.

After a lot of furious squeaking the soldiers cleared all the passengers out of three compartments and James was made to climb into one. The officer and the two air-rats came too. The engine started with a tremendous burst of waffing, but almost at once the officer insisted on tying a blindfold round James's eyes, so that he couldn't see anything at all.

He must have slept, despite the hard seat and the rat-smell, because the next thing he knew he was being prodded to his feet and pushed through the carriage door, still with the blindfold tight round his head. Rats gripped both his wrists in their teeth and hustled him through a squeaking crowd. He was hoicked up on to a sort of platform, which jerked beneath him, toppling him off his feet to the sound of squeaky rat jeers all round him. He realised that he was on the back of a lorry, guarded by rat soldiers.

The lorry roared through clattering streets. Traffic honked. A siren whooped ahead. The road was very bumpy, but it didn't last. The lorry roared for a short while over a smoother surface with no traffic near by. It halted twice while rats squeaked around. When it stopped for the third time James was lifted roughly down and the bandage taken from his eyes.

After all that darkness he blinked blindly through the glare. It wasn't daylight. The sky overhead was murky and almost dark. He must have slept all afternoon. Now he was standing in a brilliantly lit space with a great ring of lights all round. The only shadows were cast by rows of huts. As his pupils narrowed in the brightness he began to see, rising above the ring of lights, the watch-towers that guarded one of the camps where General Weil kept his prisoners. James was inside it.

Chapter 13

GENERAL WEIL

The camp was a horrible place. The only times it stopped being horrible were when James was asleep, too unhappy to dream, but even then the guards were likely to come and wake him up and make him stand by his mattress for an hour, for no reason at all. There was only the disgusting dry porridge to eat and only the foul soapy water to drink.

None of the prisoners were rats. They were other creatures of the Dump—mice, voles, toads and such— all grown large and clever in their own ways. Each sort lived in separate huts, the slow sad toads in one block, the mice in another and so on. James wasn't allowed near any of them, but from what he could see the voles were the best. There was something unbeatable about them. Though they were tottery with starvation they would never give in to the bullying guards. Even at the most terrifying moments there would be a shrill mutter some-where in the ranks, followed by a burst of scornful vole laughter. The mice tried to please the rats, cringing and creeping. It didn't do them any good. These were in the huts on either side of James. He didn't see enough of the toads and the others to know how they behaved.

He was in a tiny hut by himself. Next to it was a cage, containing two of the great gulls. When James was allowed out for exercise he would look at their grey, bedraggled plumage and their yellow untamed eyes. For some reason they gave him a kind of hope.

The worst thing wasn't the food or the loneliness or the cruel guards or the big flies flocking around like pigeons, it was the ants. Red ants, a foot high. The rats used them as guard dogs. They could bite with their huge jaws and they could spit burning acid. A guard, on purpose, put a drop of the acid on James's skin to warn him how much it hurt. It hurt all right. The ants lived in a great nest under the camp which meant that there was no hope of tunnelling out.

No hope of escape, not by any ordinary means. No hope at all. Everything had gone wrong, just when it seemed to be going so right. James kept remembering the brilliant morning when the airship had floated over Rat City and he had looked down on this very camp, off on the expedition with the Burra to find what was wrong with the Dump. Sometimes he wondered if he hadn't in fact found what was wrong, here, this foul camp. That was wrong, wasn't it? In moods like this, when he was sure the guards weren't watching, he would take his box of nothing out and turn it over and over, looking for clues to how it opened. If he could only find the secret then perhaps the nothing would come flooding out and swallow the whole terrible camp, and Rat City, and the Dump, and James would be back outside the fence with Mum shouting at him. But somehow he knew that wasn't the answer. The camp was wrong, yes, but it was only an effect, not a cause. The cause was somewhere else, and he had to get there. *Then*, perhaps, the box would be ready to open.

He made scratches in a secret place on the wall behind his mattress to help him count the days. On the twelfth morning, before it was light, there was a lot of squeaking and scurrying around, and the porridge-stuff was shoved through the door earlier than usual, and then James's guards made him sweep his hut clean and fold his blanket into a neat square and then go and stand in the space between the gulls' cage and his hut.

He waited for hours in the icy dawn while all the other prisoners were brought out and made to stand in lines. It was a sort of parade. At last, when the sun was up and James was just beginning to stop shivering, he heard a shrill fanfare of rat trumpets. The rat anthem blared from the camp loudspeakers and the guards strutted up and down with truncheons, beating any prisoners they thought weren't standing properly to attention. Several hundred smart rat soldiers marched into the space opposite the prisoners, stood to attention and presented arms. A big open car rolled into sight, driven by a chauffeur with an armed guard beside him. In the back seat lolled a small grey rat wearing an enormous cap covered with gold braid. It was General Weil.

The General got out of the car and inspected his soldiers. Senior officers walked respectfully behind him. He crossed the space and began to inspect the prisoners, not really bothering to look at them but chatting over his shoulder to the officers, who answered with smarmy rat snickers. Sometimes the General rubbed his paws together or smoothed his white whiskers. James guessed he was really enjoying himself, strolling round like this in front of his prisoners. A bit like Grandad taking people round his garden.

When the General reached the gull-cage he stopped. This was what he had come for. He looked fiercely at the gulls and began to squeak. Soon he was jumping up and down in excitement, the way all the rats seemed to, only more so. He shrilled and spat until there was froth on his whiskers. He was terrifying, a mad little old rat who could do what he liked with everyone. With James.

At last he moved on. He was probably still in a bit of a daze after using all that energy yelling at the gulls, because he went straight past James without noticing him, but one of his officers caught him up and said something very respectfully and he stopped, stared and came back. His whiskers quivered. He squeaked a question and an

officer answered. He came closer, wrinkling his nose. James could smell his ratty breath. His mean little eyes under the huge cap were as sharp as pins. He put out a paw and prodded James's chest. He snickered. Then his expression changed.

He snapped an order. James's guards seized his arms. An officer came forward and tried to open James's anorak. He didn't understand about the zip, but he got it loose in the end and pulled the anorak open. General Weil darted in with a quick rat rush and put his paw into James's inside pocket, which was just where he had prodded the anorak from the outside. He must have felt that there was something there then. The box of nothing. He snatched it out.

And it worked.

One moment there was the dreadful ruler of Rat City standing in the middle of his prison camp with his soldiers behind him, and the next there was nothing but a huge gold-braided cap lying on the ground, jiggling as the rat trapped under it tried to get out.

James knew exactly what to do without having to think about it. His guards had let go of his arms in their astonishment, so he pounced, grabbed both sides of the cap, squeezed them together till he could hold them in one hand, and then with his other hand pulled the wriggling creature out and held it up by the nape of its neck.

The camp seemed to go mad. The rat soldiers stood and stared, and so did the guards, but the ants came swarming out of their nest and ran about biting and spitting among the ranks. The voles rushed at the soldiers and wrestled their guns away. The rats were three times their size and outnumbered them too, but they just let it happen. They could easily have jumped on James and rescued their leader, but it was as though the whole of Rat City depended so much on him that if he wasn't there to give the orders none of the others dared do anything.

The voles formed themselves into squads and rushed

the main gates. The toads thumped off after them without saying thank you to anyone. The mice stayed in their ranks, trembling, but after a while they crept away too. James was left alone with the rat which had been General Weil dangling from his right hand.

But not quite alone. There were still the gulls in their cage, watching everything with their wild haughty look as though it was no affair of theirs at all. James picked up his box of nothing, walked across to the cage and pressed it against the lock. By the time he had put the box back in his pocket the whole cage had tinkled into rusty scraps, which the gulls shook from their backs. They strutted a few steps, stretched their wings and folded them again.

"Go on," said James. "They'll come to their senses any moment."

One gull turned its head, stalked across, picked James up in its beak by the collar of his anorak and dumped him on the other gull's back. He scrabbled for a hold as the great wings stretched again. He needed both hands, so he couldn't help letting go of the rat which had been General Weil. It leaped for the ground as the gull took off.

Soon they were skimming above the roofs of Rat City. The streets were in turmoil, with barricades blazing at every corner. Nobody bothered about a couple of gulls flying over.

Chapter 14

GULL COUNTRY

"We thought we might not see you again," said the Burra.

"Were you worried?"

"Not really. We did not think any harm could come to you while you had your box, but we passed a motion expressing our regret."

"Oh."

The gulls had left James on a high cliff ledge with no way up or down. The Burra was there already, with some of the junk from the airship. The airship itself was moored at another ledge, a bit along the cliff. It looked decidedly floppy after all the gas it had lost, and was only just buoyant even without its load. On the other side of the vast shadowy valley the peaks of a mountain glittered in the sunset. At this height the air was biting, so James found a blanket and wrapped it round his anorak. He'd been thrilled to see the Burra again, but now, after the excitement of the escape from the camp, he felt a bit of a let-down. And when the Burra said it hadn't even been worried! That wasn't fair. James knew he'd had a perfectly foul time. The Burra didn't understand. Losing James was probably only like losing the leg the rat patrol had shot up, a bit of a pity, that's all.

James was brooding on the unfairness when he felt his blanket stir, rumple itself, and rub gently against his cheek like a purring cat. He realised the Burra did understand a bit, in its own way. At least it knew what it was like to be scared sick, because of its battle with the biplane.

"What about you," he said. "Are you all right?"

"We are so-so. It was all something of a shock. We remember very little about it. We were all taken up with hanging together."

"Was it the computer did that?"

"Oh no. It was us. All of us."

"It practically blew itself up, fighting the biplane. I'm surprised it's still working."

The computer, with the small portable TV which was its display screen now, lay on the ledge with the other

oddments from the airship. Its case looked a bit gone, not quite straight anywhere any longer, but the "On" light was glowing and the pink heart shone as if it had just been painted.

"Working?" said the Burra. "Playing, more like it!"

"Space Invaders, you mean?"

"Not that either. It . . . hello!"

The screen had lit up with a mass of figures and letters and symbols, line after line of them. The lines began to move, dancing around, and as they danced the figures and symbols changed and vanished, sometimes in pairs, sometimes several at a time, until there was only one line left.

"That is the computer's idea of a game," said the Burra. "It does not mean a thing to the rest of us."

"Nor me, neither," said James. "But it's sort of neat, isn't it?"

(Maths was the part of school he liked best. Mrs Last

gave him sums of his own because he was way ahead of the rest of the class.)

"The universe came out of a sum like that, you know?" he said. "I saw it on TV, the night before . . . before all this started. And in the end it will go back into a sum. The universe, I mean."

"That does not help us to get our knots re-tied."

"Are they bad? Can't you just do it by guess-work?"

"We unravelled into some quite big holes. The trouble is that if we get one knot slightly wrong it puts the others out and the net is the wrong shape. It must be a smooth curve or we will not fly straight. So we keep having to go back and try again. The computer could work it all out for us if it chose to, but it seems to think its game is more important."

"Perhaps it is, only we don't know. When you finish mending yourself can we just go?"

"There are two problems. First we must find a fresh supply of gas. Second, we will need the gulls' permission. We are their prisoner, you see. They have not yet worked out that we are all one creature. If we had more gas the airship could join the rest of us and we might escape by night, but the gulls could easily overtake us next day. Our forcefield modulaters are beyond repair, and in any case they depend on the computer to operate them."

"Am I a prisoner too, now?"

"We are afraid so."

"I don't think that's fair, after what I did for them."

"Perhaps they will take that into account. They seem to have a highly developed sense of honour. Overdeveloped, you might almost say."

"What do you mean?"

"Well, some of their behaviour is extremely ridiculous, but we strongly advise you not to laugh at them."

It was a bore being a prisoner again, though at least the food was better and there was the Burra to talk to. But there seemed to be even less chance of getting away from this high, cold ledge than there had been from General Weil's camp, and all so far from home, and Floral Street, and the family. James was feeling pretty depressed when, half way through next morning, he heard a whoosh and a thump and there was one of the great gulls ruffling its feathers into place on the rim of the ledge.

The gull didn't do anything. It just stood there, facing out over the cliff edge. If you want to show how haughty you are, James thought, standing still is a good way. Ordinary seaside gulls do a lot of that, on flagpoles and statues and things, but they do quite a bit of quarrelling too. A quarrel between two of these monsters, with their big tearing beaks, would be something to see.

He was wondering about that when there was another whoosh as a gull swooped by and without landing plucked the Burra off the ledge by one ear. The first gull stalked over to James, pecked down, grabbed him by the scruff of his anorak and launched itself out over the valley. No please or do-you-mind or anything like that, oh no. James could see the Burra dangling from the other gull's beak a hundred yards ahead. He only hoped the ear would stand the strain.

They swung out round a jut of the mountain and then in towards a great curve of cliff where hundreds of the huge gulls roosted on different ledges. James could see nests with fluffy young in them, and others where a parent sat on eggs, just like ordinary gulls. The only difference was that a place like this at the seaside in the real world would have been deafening with squawks and squabbles. Here it was almost silent.

They landed on a large ledge where a dozen other gulls were waiting. The birds who had brought them put James and the Burra down and stalked over to join their comrades. All the gulls stood quite still. James couldn't even guess whether they were watching him—a bird's eye is different from an animal's. You can tell where an animal is looking, you can't with a bird. He didn't think he liked the gulls much. They were beautiful, but dangerous. He'd hated the rats but he'd been able to understand them, guess what they were thinking and feeling. He hadn't a clue with the gulls.

"What's happening?" he whispered.

"We do not know. Stand still. Stare back at them. And whatever you do, do not laugh."

"Fat chance."

So James stood and stared. He tried to imagine what it was like to be a gull, to feel as haughty and fierce as that, Emperor James, ruler of the universe, terror of the skyways, etcetera etcetera. The gulls didn't seem to notice but it made him feel better. At last they moved, closing into a ring with their beaks inward, and began a soft bubbling noise, gull talk, probably.

"Smell anything?" muttered the Burra.

James sniffed. There was a proper pong—just what you'd expect coming from beneath a cliff where gulls had been nesting for years.

"We could fractionate some gas out of there," said the Burra.

"Wouldn't you need the computer?"

"Luckily the equipment has come along as a member of the expedition."

"You've still got to persuade the gulls."

"Shh. Something is happening."

The circle of gulls was breaking apart to form an arc facing James and the Burra. The gull in the centre stepped forward. It was slightly larger than the others, and haughtier, and fiercer-looking. It bent its head, pecked something off the ledge and came forward carrying in its beak what looked like a hairy caterpillar, very dead and floppy. Gull food? A peace offering? Were they going to have to eat . . .?

The gull laid the offering at the Burra's feet.

"Why! It is our old leg!" said the Burra.

It was indeed—the camel-leg which had been shot half to pieces by the rat patrol on James's first evening in the Dump, and then been nicked by a gull. The gulls must have realised it had something to do with the Burra and now they were giving it back.

At the sound of the Burra's voice the leg twitched.

And James laughed.

Once he'd started he couldn't stop. Partly it was sheer relief at not having to eat a hairy caterpillar, partly it was pleasure at getting the leg back—he'd always worried about it slightly, in the back of his mind—but mainly it was the sight of that great proud bird facing the idiotic-looking Burra and giving it its own leg as a present. James hadn't had much to laugh at for quite a long time, and now it felt as though a fortnight's supply was coming out in one go.

Gulls have no sense of humour, none at all, which makes it hard to understand how this gull knew what the noise James was making meant, but it did. It turned slowly towards James, stared at him and then stalked away. At the same time another gull walked over and picked the Burra up by its ear, carried it along the ledge and dumped it in the middle of the circle of birds. James rushed to follow, but one of the gulls immediately grabbed him by his anorak and tossed him clear. Between the yellow legs James could see the Burra waving its arms about, trying to explain something in sign language. Nothing else happened for a long while, and then the circle broke up and the Burra came over.

"This is somewhat serious," it said.

"I'm sorry. I couldn't help it."

"No doubt."

"What's going to happen?"

"Well, it is up to you, James. As far as we can make out, the gulls could not at first decide whether we counted as a rat or a gull. That is how they think. When you rescued two of them from the camp, they decided we

must be gulls. But now that you have insulted them by laughing at one of their chieftains they think we may be rats after all. If we are gulls they will help us on our way, but if we are rats they will take us back into rat country and leave us there."

"They can't! How can we show them?"

"You can show them by doing what one gull does when it has insulted another. You can, if you are willing, agree to fight a duel."

"All right," said James, without even thinking.

Chapter 15

DUEL

"We have seen this going on several times," said the Burra. "But we have not understood what was happening. It was too far off. It is how they avoid continual quarrels, of course."

"I suppose so," said James. He was feeling too sick with fright to think about it. The way duels worked in gull country was a bit like old-fashioned duelling with pistols, except the gulls hadn't got pistols so they took in turn to drop rocks on each other. There were special rules about how far apart they had to be, and so on. There was even a rule about what happened when one of the duellists couldn't fly—because it had broken a wing-bone in an earlier duel, for instance. They were using this rule for James. He and the Burra, who was his second, were waiting on a special ledge where the cliff sloped away above so that a gull could fly directly over it to drop its rocks; the ledge was on an overhang, so that the gull could go down and circle almost directly below when it was its turn to have rocks dropped on it.

"It is rather a sensible system, in its way," said the Burra.

"I think it's absolutely stupid," said James. "I think the gulls are even stupider than the rats."

"We think you will be very unlucky to be hit," said the Burra. "You are a smaller target than a gull. We

93

offered to let the challenger fly lower to take that into account . . ."

"You did what!"

"Well, we decided it was more honourable. Remember we are trying to prove you are not a rat. And we also thought that if we did not offer they might ask, but if we did offer they would feel honour bound to refuse."

"Thanks a lot."

"Ah, it looks as though we are ready. You drop first."

"I'm going to aim to miss."

"Oh, no. Most unwise. An added insult. This is serious, James."

"You're telling me!"

A gull swooped down to the ledge and collected the Burra, who waved good luck as it was carried away. James went to the edge of the ledge and picked up one of the rocks that had been laid ready there. There were six of them, three each, about the size of tennis balls. If one of those landed on your head from a height it would smash right through. Gulls broke wings in duels, didn't they? That showed.

He looked over the dizzy drop. Down there his opponent was circling, close against the cliff. He tried to make his mind do sums. If he aimed where the bird was now, how far would it have flown by the time the stone reached it? He had to miss, but not too badly. The sums wouldn't work. On ledges and crags all around other gulls were gathered, like spectators at a snooker match, silent, intense. At last the signal came, one harsh squawk from the umpire. James took his time, making sure they all saw he was doing his best to hit. He almost did, too, much nearer than he meant. The rock whistled down inches beside the bird's head. The bird sailed smoothly on as though nothing had happened.

Another squawk and it was James's turn to be the target. His opponent came soaring up to the ledge, picked up a stone in its beak without landing or looking at James and spiralled on into the sky.

James began to walk round and round in a small circle, imitating the way the gull had flown below. He held his head back and looked straight in front of him, but inside he was really scared. It wasn't like falling out of the airship or being captured by the rats, or even meeting General Weil. Then everything had been sudden and strange and he hadn't really understood what he was frightened of. This time he knew exactly. A rock was going to fall out of the sky and if it hit him it would smash his head in. And he mustn't look up, or dodge, or flinch. Just walk steadily round and round.

Smack! The rock slapped into the ledge a couple of paces ahead of him. He hadn't even heard the signal squawk.

While he waited for his opponent to take its place again below James looked at the rock he was going to throw. It was just like an ordinary big flint, the sort you could pick up in a field. He remembered what had happened to the rat bullets when he'd found the dying gull by the stream and touched it with the box of nothing. Suppose he were to put the box on his head while he was walking round . . .

Just to see, he took the box out and tried it on the rock. Nothing much happened. The change wasn't in the stone, but in the way he was looking at it. It was still a flint, but now he noticed that all along one side two lines of flakes had been carefully chipped away in a sort of pattern, leaving an edge that was sharp enough to cut your finger if you weren't careful. An old flint axe, or something. He'd seen ones like it on school visits to the museum. If *that* landed on your nut . . .

Dimly he heard the signal to fire. Without even bothering to aim he tossed the rock away. He was still in the daze of horror when all round him the cliff rang with gull-cries. Now he looked over the edge and saw his opponent breaking from the circle and beginning to fly up, while two or three white feathers floated away on the breeze. This time the gull landed on the ledge and looked at James with its fierce, proud stare. Slowly it lowered its head. James put his right arm in front of his waist and bowed, the way he'd learnt to for last term's form play. The gull bowed again.

They went on bobbing up and down to each other, the way gulls do sometimes, until several more gulls landed on the ledge, one of them bringing the Burra.

"Well done," said the Burra. "They seem to have decided that your coolness under fire shows you are a gull after all."

"Did I hurt the one I hit?"

"A glancing blow only. Most satisfactory."

"When can we go? I don't like it here. I want to get moving."

"About two days, if all goes well."

"Great!"

Chapter 16

THE DESERT

It was marvellous to be flying again, drifting on the same steady wind, not so strong as it had been by the shore but still pushing the airship on above the glittering mountain peaks. Two or three gulls were usually circling round as an escort.

"They're not so bad when they're flying," said James. "Friendly of them to come with us."

"Or perhaps they want to make sure we go right away," said the Burra.

"Do you think they know why the Dump's gone wrong? I mean, they could have flown off exploring miles and miles."

"We tried to ask them. Not easy in sign language. They did not understand, in any case. We doubt if it is the sort of thing gulls think about."

"But we're still going the right way? You can feel it?"

"Oh yes. And have you not noticed—everything is getting older?"

James knew what the Burra meant. The shore where he'd landed was covered with the rubbish of the world he knew. Further inland, when he'd fallen out of the airship, the hill had been made of older kinds of stuff. And then among the gulls he'd seen the stone axe, which must have been thousands of years old.

"We think we are going back to the beginning," said the Burra.

"The beginning of the Dump, you mean?"

"The beginning of everything."

"That's stupid. You have to have people to make rubbish. There weren't any people then."

"Oh no. Everything becomes rubbish in the end. We sometimes wonder if people weren't invented as an extra-quick way of making rubbish."

During the third night, while James was sleeping, they left the mountains. He woke and saw the huge blue wall of them, already miles behind. The gulls were gone too. Below, and on both sides, and as far as he could see ahead, was desert—endless, rolling dunes, the colour of cinders, like vast sea waves, stuck. Not a tree or a bush anywhere, of course.

They floated on all morning and it was still the same. The dunes were not like real desert because they were all exactly the same shape. You could follow one into the distance until your eyes ached and there was no change in it, no break or fork, not even a dip or hummock. You couldn't look at them for long. Their size and sameness were not just boring, they were frightening. It was also incredibly hot, even in the shadow of the gas-bag. The sunlight bounced roasting off the mottled grey surface below and because the airship was moving at the same speed as the wind there wasn't a breeze to cool you. The Burra was too busy keeping the airship working without the computer's help to talk much.

The only slightly amusing thing that happened all day was that James found out the computer was interested in his box of nothing. He'd noticed that it usually gave a few extra bips and blinks when he came near; when he got the box out to have another try at finding out how it was supposed to open the computer became almost excited, and only quieted down when he put the box away.

Towards sunset it got cool enough to move about again. With the sun so low the lines of the dunes stood out more sharply because of the shadows between them. They didn't run in a dead straight line, but curved ever so slightly forward on both sides of the airship. Looking back at the glittering peaks, still just visible above the horizon, James got the idea that they weren't a straight line either, but ran in an enormous curve, like the dunes. Suppose all these curves went on and on, then they'd meet somewhere hundreds of miles ahead. They'd all be parts of enormous circles, one inside the other. And at the middle, what? It reminded James of something. He got it in the end.

"Burra," he said. "There's been a splash."

"A splash?"

"Like when you throw a stone in a pond. Ripples. Look."

"We believe you may be right. How interesting."

"I've seen pictures like this on TV, only not so big. Where a meteorite has smashed into the Earth. You get a crater, and ripples."

"I see. So what we have to do is cross the dunes at right angles all the time, and then we must be heading towards the centre."

"I suppose so. It must have been jainormous, whatever it was made the splash. A whole comet or something."

The dunes had become interesting all of a sudden. James knelt with his elbows on the rim of the basket and watched them gliding backwards. Each circle had got to be a bit smaller than the one before, to fit inside it. They were huge right out here, so big that you could only just see that they curved at all, but if you went on they would get smaller and smaller, until . . .

There ought to be a sum for working out how far it was to the middle. James tried to think about it, but Mrs Last hadn't taught him that kind of maths yet. He pulled the sheet of paper out of his pocket. He didn't want to spoil his picture of the star-tree so he turned it over and drew some circles on the back, inside each other like a target. He stared at the paper. It was still too difficult.

He put the paper away and looked at the dunes again. You had to have some extra measurements. Suppose you chose a place right out along one of the dunes and guessed how far away it was, and then you measured the distance it took the airship to get exactly at right angles to it . . .

The trouble was choosing a place. There wasn't anything to make one bit of a dune different from anywhere else on all the other dunes. The moment you looked away you'd lost it. At least it was better trying now than in the middle of the day. Every bump on the surface cast a long, hard shadow. There ought to be something . . .

There! That line! That was different. No it wasn't. Hey!

"Burra! Look! Something's been there!"

"Where, James?"

"A sort of trail. Can't you see? It goes across that dune, and the one before and the one after."

The Burra screwed in a long-distance eye and peered.

"We believe you may be right," it said. "We had better go and have a look. Not enough time to drift over before the sun goes down."

As it spoke the engine rattled into life, the propeller whupped and the airship swung sideways on to the wind, nudging its way across until it was directly over the marks James had seen. By now only the topmost ridges of the dunes were still in sunlight, but the marks were there all right, though you probably wouldn't have noticed them at all if it hadn't been for the shadows they cast in the sideways light. There was a shallow, scuffled trail on either side of a deeper groove, which ran in a straight line over dune after dune. James and the Burra were still gazing down at the marks when the sun left the ground and the shadows vanished. For a few minutes more the airship drifted along in sunlight, and then the shadow of the world swept up and covered it.

"I think it's a dinosaur," said James. "If you're right about things getting older, I mean. The middle bit is where it drags its tail, and the outside ones are where it pushes itself along with its feet. I'd like to meet a dinosaur."

"The footmarks would be clearer."

"Several dinosaurs then, scuffling each other's foot-marks out."

"Possibly. We will look again in the morning."

The desert stars came out, too big to be real. It was night almost at once. Soon the moon rose and James could see the dunes again, vast curves of dead grey with black valleys between. It got very cold, so he let his blankets wrap themselves round him and dropped asleep without noticing. He dreamed he was escaping from a Tyrannosaurus Rex, so next morning he wasn't sure he wanted to meet a dinosaur after all.

The tracks had gone. Perhaps the creature had stopped in the night. Or else the wind had drifted the airship off course. Yes. If you looked carefully you could see that the curve of the dunes was different on different sides of the airship, because it was no longer crossing them at right angles. So they'd not just lost the tracks, they weren't heading for the centre of the splash any more.

"It is all right," said the Burra. "We will adjust with our fins. It is not worth using fuel."

So most of the day they drifted slantwise to the wind, which meant there was a slight breeze across the basket, so it was cooler than yesterday. About the middle of the afternoon the Burra said, "Look, there are your tracks."

With the sun at that angle you could only just see them by the faint lines they made across the dunes ahead and behind. Directly underneath the airship they were invisible.

"It's funny they want to go the same way as we do," said James.

"It is peculiar," said the Burra, "but it may not be funny."

"What do you mean?"

"We are guessing."

It turned out a good guess. Towards evening they floated over one of the valleys between the dunes, all just the same as each other, and saw that it was different. There was a dark splodge on the upward slope. The airship's pumps started, sucking gas out of the bag so that they could drift gently lower. As it came nearer the splodge stirred and broke apart, letting James see that it was a swarm of the horrible Dump flies feeding on something they'd found—a huge dead lizard. The flies were like vultures round a carcase on a real desert.

"That's what made the tracks," said James. "It probably came here to die, like a sort of lizard's graveyard."

"But the tracks go on."

They did, too, straight up the dune and over the ridge as though nothing had happened.

"We think we ought to investigate," said the Burra.

"Do you want me to go down?"

"Yes, please. We will take all precautions."

The airship lowered a couple of anchors which burrowed into the ground like moles. A rope uncoiled and knotted itself round James's chest and shoulders. He climbed over the side of the basket and let go. The rope took his weight without a jerk and let him gently down to the ground, but stayed in its knots, ready to hoick him back up if anything went wrong.

The ground was roasting hot, even through his shoes. It crunched like loose cinders as he walked over to the dead lizard. The flies rose with an angry buzz. Just where they had clustered thickest, at the back of the lizard's head, there was a neat round hole. James took his box of nothing out of his pocket and placed it against the lizard's body. His idea was that it might do the same trick as it had with the wounded gull, though he didn't think it would work with a dead animal.

It didn't, not like that. The body, which had been as long as three cars, bumper to bumper, shrank in a blink. James stood looking down at the bare white bones of a lizard, about a foot long. When he touched them with his foot they fell apart, as if they had been lying there for ages.

The flies hazed to and fro, baffled by the disappearance of their meal. Several of them settled a little way off and began to feed on something else. James trudged across to look.

On the cindery ground there was a scattering of something softer and paler grey. He picked up a few of the flakes, looked at them, smelt them. He knew what they were, only too well. They were the stuff he had been given to eat in General Weil's camp, the stuff the soldiers had eaten too. Rat food.

Chapter 17

THE RACE IS ON

"And the lizard had been shot," said James.

"You are sure?" said the Burra.

"I don't see it could've been anything else. Even before I saw the rat food I knew it had been shot."

"Rats, then. And more than one lizard."

"It's an expedition, you see. The lizards belong in the desert. Like camels. The rats use them for carrying things. When they get sick or something the rats just shoot them and go on."

The Burra paused even longer than usual.

"We think we had better start the engine," it said.

"What about getting back?"

"We will have to think about that. But it is important to get there first. We don't know why. It is just a feeling. We belong to the Dump, remember. We feel what it feels. That is how we knew it had ceased to function. Now we know we must get there before the rats."

"Oh, all right. Anyway it's boring, just drifting. Let's go."

The engine chuttered awake as the anchors undug themselves. Now the breeze seemed to come from dead ahead, roasting hot but better than stillness. The dunes slid by at triple speed. Though there was nothing new to see, it was exciting, and part of the excitement was knowing that if the wind did drop, or they ran out of fuel, there was absolutely no way they would ever walk all those miles back to safety across the scorching cinders. They would die in the desert, and nothing would save them.

The sun went down and the stars came out. James slept, but the engine battered away all night, and when he woke in the morning he was quite certain he could see that the curve of the dunes was sharper than it had been the day before. The circles must still be immense, but they were getting slowly smaller as the airship drove towards their centre.

Towards evening they came to another dead lizard. The Burra agreed there was no special point in landing, but pumped gas to skim lower over the spot. On the slope beyond the lizard, to one side of the trail, was a small white dot. As they came nearer James saw it was balanced on a sort of stalk, like a peculiar desert flower. The airship swooped past, only a few feet away, and now he could see what it really was. The white bit was a sun-helmet, the old-fashioned sort explorers used to wear. The stalk was a rifle stuck in the ground. At its foot was a narrow mound, a grave.

But still the tracks went straight on. In the shadow-casting evening light the lizards' footprints were clearly marked on either side of the groove where they dragged their tails.

"I think there's only two left," James said.

"So do we. The question is, how far ahead are they?"

"It can't be too far. I mean, if that first one had been killed weeks ago the flies wouldn't have been interested in it. We must be going faster than they are now. How far do you think it is to the middle? I've been trying to do the sum. I think I can see a way but I don't know how the maths is supposed to work."

He got out his picture and showed the Burra the circles he'd drawn on the back, and the lines he'd put in. The Burra grunted. It was the sort of sum the computer could have done in a thousandth of a second, but there was no point in asking it. The Burra had to think it out. James counted ridges and helped guess distances. From time to time he heard a calculator blipping inside the duffel-bag under the Burra's sailor-shirt.

"We have had to do a lot of guessing," said the Burra at last. "Some time tomorrow, we think."

"Have you got enough fuel?"

"Yes, if the wind holds."

James slept. All night the engine muttered through his dreams. They were nightmares, mostly. One was about General Weil, wearing a sun-helmet and whipping his great lizard across the dunes. He had a chain-saw strapped to his saddle, because at the dead centre there grew the only tree in all this world, a marvellous star-tree, and General Weil was going to cut it down and bring all the stars crashing out of the sky. He had to be stopped. James was on his bike, whizzing along, but then he was trying to force his wheels through soft sand, and then the bicycle melted away and he was plodding up a slithering dune and the flies were buzzing and muttering all around, waiting for him to die. And then he woke up. That was typical, but he had several of that sort of dream.

When he woke in the morning the first thing he did was look at the dunes. The curve was clearly there now, easy to see from the height at which the airship flew. For a moment he thought the tracks had vanished and they'd passed the rat expedition in the night, but then he saw them, only a faint dotted line. No lizard footprints, no central groove.

"They've left the lizards behind," he said. "They're going on on foot."

"Yes," said the Burra. "Just two of them, we think."

"They must be incredibly brave. How far to the middle now?"

"About twelve hours."

"I thought you said before that."

"The wind is dying. It is hardly helping us at all."

"Oh. Are you going to have enough fuel?"

"Perhaps."

As the sun rose the tracks vanished. James only knew they were still following them when, about mid-day, they passed another grave, marked like the first one with a helmet and rifle, but dug so shallow that the tip of the rat's tail stuck out of the cinders. He went to the front of the basket and stared across the burning dunes. Even in the shadow of the gas-bag the heat was dreadful. The breeze the airship made as it pushed along was like the rush of hot air you feel if someone opens an oven and you're standing too close. But the curve of the dunes had become so strong that James could see they really were like the rings of an enormous target. And the bull's-eye had to be somewhere dead ahead. There.

If it had been the star-tree he'd dreamed about he'd have seen it by now. He screwed up his eyes and stared through the glare across the narrowing rings. Was there something there? A sort of darker patch?

Knowing how far it was made the airship seem to go slower. You could watch time pass by the way the shadow of the gas-bag sidled across the dunes. At first it was over to the left. At mid-day it was right underneath. An hour later it was a bit to the right. Then it was more than twice as far.

It was about there when James saw the explorer. Or
rather he saw a white dot near the ridge of one of the
dunes a long way in front. It vanished over the top, and
the airship drove on. Quite a long time later he saw it
again, and a dark shape beneath it struggling slowly up
over the cinders. Next time it came into sight it was
obviously a rat wearing a sun-helmet. The airship had
crossed nine ridges while the rat was moving from one
to the next. In fact they would catch up while it was still
on this ridge.

At first the rat seemed not to notice the airship, but
continued to struggle up the slope. You could see from
the way it moved that it was totally exhausted with heat
and effort, but still somehow driving itself on. It seemed
to hear the engine for the first time as it paused for a
moment to rest at the top of the dune.

The rat turned and looked back at the sky, shading its eyes with one paw. It unslung its rifle and waited. When the airship came in range it started to shoot, but it was so tired that the barrel rocked to and fro and most of the shots went wild. A few may have hit the gas-bag, but if so the Burra sealed them almost at once.

As the airship sailed by James saw that the explorer was a large rat with almost black fur, nothing like horrible General Weil. He knew it would have killed him if it could, and killed the Burra too—supposing there was any way you could kill something like the Burra—rather than let them reach the centre first, but even so he felt sorry for it. It had tried so hard and got so far. When they were out of range it slung its rifle on to its back and started on all fours down the next slope.

Now from this height he could see the centre. Or rather he could see where it was. The sun was shining slantwise again, and the ridged rings stood out strongly with the shadows between them. He could see their far sides dwindling into the distance. At the very heart was something like a huge pool.

Done it, he thought. We'll be first. We should be there before the sun goes down.

The thought was still in his mind when the engine coughed, stopped, started, coughed twice and stopped completely.

"Out of fuel," said the Burra.

"We're almost there. We can just drift. The rat can't possibly catch up."

James watched a ridge below slide backwards, slow as dreams. The valley took an age to cross. Directly over the next ridge the airship stopped completely.

"No wind," said the Burra.

Chapter 18

THE BOX OPENS

The sun went down through bars of scarlet. The airship hung in stillness. Nothing moved. It was as though the black pool made the stillness, stopping the wind which had blown so steadily across the desert from ever quite reaching it. Suddenly the light left the ridges of the dunes and all the desert was in shadow. James stopped watching out aft to see how the rat was getting on. It had crossed three ridges since the airship stopped. There were four before it caught up and then six more to the black centre.

"Can't you wiggle your fins and sort of row us forward?" he said.

"It may be worth a try," said the Burra.

James heard a gentle swishing noise overhead. Slowly the airship swung round until it was facing the way they had come. The last rim of the sun dipped out of sight and at the same moment shadow swept up and covered the gas-bag. Stars came out like lights being turned on. The airship was still over the same dune.

"I know," said James. "If you go lower you can let me down on a rope like you did when I went to look at the lizard. I'll tow you."

"Do you think you can?"

"We've got to get there first."

The moment his shoes touched the cinders James started down the slope with the rope still knotted to his shoulders. His feet made rattling little avalanches at each step. Above him he could hear a different rattle and slither as every strand of cord the Burra could spare undid itself and then knotted itself to his line. The longer the better. There was no point in trying to tow until he was well up the far slope, because he'd mainly be pulling downwards.

At last he crossed the valley floor and started to climb. It was just like his dream, step after plodding step with the cinders slithering back beneath his weight so that it was like trying to run up a down escalator. Still no use pulling, because that would just drag him back and down instead of hauling the airship forward. The weight of the rope began to be a nuisance. He gave up trying to climb straight and zig-zagged instead, though at the end of each zig he was only a few feet higher than the last one. The dune was like a mountain. And the explorer rat had four feet. Much easier like that. It could probably climb straight. If it could cross two dunes while he was crossing one it would catch him up.

The thought drove him desperately on. Long after his legs had become floppy bags of jelly they kept moving somehow while his lungs sucked at the crackling dusty air. At last the slope eased and he could climb straight. On, on. He staggered to the top and turned to pull. He wouldn't be able to do the next ridge, not without a rest.

The moon had risen, full and bright. The airship glistened like a sleeping fish in the black of the night. James gripped the rope to haul it in, but as soon as he had his feet firm it started hauling of its own accord from the other end, pulling so hard that he had to lean right back, like in tug-of-war.

The Burra was right. It was that first bit of pull when the rope was almost level, that was what mattered. The closer the airship got the more it would waste energy just pulling down, not longways. But the Burra judged its course beautifully, pumping gas so that it could swoop down directly towards James and skimming the basket past so close he could have put up his hand and touched it.

"Run and jump when I call!" shouted the Burra as it whistled by.

James turned. The Burra was pumping gas the other way now, making its flight curve upwards. The rope was paying itself out. He got ready. The Burra's grating cry floated across the night.

"Now!"

James ran, sprinting across the clogging cinders. The rope kept pace, so that it hung in an easy curve between him and the airship. The slope dipped down, steeper and steeper.

"Jump!" shouted the Burra.

It was more of a stagger than a leap, but it was something, a forward effort, and he was in the air. The rope had tightened at the last moment and now he was swooping through the air like Tarzan on a creeper, with the wind whistling round him, out and down across the valley, faster and faster, and then up, slower now, and landing with a soft thump sprawling on cinders well up the next slope.

He flung out his arms and legs, spreading himself as wide as he could to stop himself slipping down. Carefully he rose to his feet and started to climb. Much better than last time, most of the steep part done for him, but still harder work than he'd ever done in his life. If it hadn't been so important—he didn't know why—he would have lain down on the cinders and given up. It wouldn't have been fair, asking him to kill himself, almost, climbing and hauling like that. But it was.

Slowly he staggered the last few steps to the top of the next ridge, turned, and dug his feet into the cinders ready to be the anchor by which the airship could haul itself forward and on. The Burra seemed to understand how tired he was. Perhaps it could feel his feelings along the rope. Anyway, it gave him a bit of a rest before the rope tightened. As he stood there, gasping and shivering, a movement caught his eye. Not on the ridge he had just left, but the one beyond. For a few seconds a white spot gleamed in the moonlight, with a darkness below it too large to be its shadow. The thing scuttled across the cinders and vanished into the valley. In that moment the whole urgency of the race came back into James's mind. He forgot his tiredness and leaned against the pull of the tautening rope, trying to hurry the airship on.

"That rat's only one ridge behind," he called as the airship skimmed past. "He's running!"

"We know," called the Burra. "We are just keeping pace. Ready? Now!"

Knowing what it was going to be like James managed the Tarzan bit much better this time, and the Burra had had some practice too. James landed further up the next dune and managed not to slither at all. So they moved on. Swoop, scramble, haul. Swoop, scramble, haul. The swoops were exciting, and the hauling bits weren't too bad, but the scrambling slithering climb seemed worse and worse, even though the Burra was landing him further up the dune each time. Only the thought of the rat scuttling along behind kept him going. That rat, he knew, had crossed hundreds of miles of desert. Its companions had died, and so had its lizards. It had trav-elled on foot over the burning cinders for a whole long day. And still, somehow, it was managing to run. General

Weil didn't deserve to have a rat like that exploring for him. He didn't see it again, but the Burra did. They were just keeping pace.

The Burra counted the ridges still to go. There had been six when James had started to tow the airship. Four, three, two, last one. . . . He staggered to the top of the ridge, turned, dug his heels in, hauled just as before, and then as the airship swooped by he turned again, ran and leaped . . .

Out over nothing. Out over an enormous blackness, with the rope lifting him in towards the swaying basket while the pumps chuckered away shoving gas into the bag so that the airship would float up as well as out. He scrambled over the edge of the basket and sat down.

"Whew!" he said.

His legs were like cold plasticine and he went on shivering with exhaustion even after his blankets had slithered along to wrap themselves round him. As soon as the basket had stopped swinging about he crawled to its side and looked over the edge.

The blackness was a hole, but there was no bottom to it, and no sides.

The moon was well up by now. If the hole had been an ordinary crater, however deep and still, you would have seen a bit of its edges, cliffs going down into shadow, with a glimmer or two below. But there wasn't anything, only blackness.

The hole was bigger than itself. If you looked at its edges, where the last circle of dune sloped down to it, it was about a mile across. But when you looked down into it you could see—although you couldn't actually see anything—you could see that it was much, much bigger than that. Inside, it went on for ever.

And it was still, far stiller than a stone or a pool. Stiller than empty sky. The stars in the sky flung their light out at 186,000 miles a second, but when the light hit the hole it stopped moving. It became nothing.

It became part of the nothing which the crater was. The original nothing, which was there before anything was there, like he'd told the man in the Nothing Shop. The same sort of nothing he'd got in his box.

This was where the box belonged. He took it out of his anorak pocket and looked at it in the moonlight. It hadn't changed.

"What d'you suppose I'm supposed to do?" he said. "Just drop it in?"

"We don't know," said the Burra. "There is not much time. That rat is almost at the last ridge."

"I'm sure I'm supposed to open it first."

James was kneeling in the silence, twisting and tugging at the box as he'd done so often before, when he heard music. It was all on one note, the usual computer bleep, but it had a dancing sort of rhythm, like a song that suddenly comes into your mind when you thought you'd forgotten it. The computer's indicator-light was shining extra bright.

"Well, someone is happy," said the Burra. It produced its grating laugh and patted the computer casing in a friendly way.

"Oh," it said.

In the silence and stillness you noticed every movement. James wasn't looking that way, but suddenly he saw the explorer's white sun-helmet gleam on the last ridge. He was just going to call out when he felt the Burra's furry, fingerless paw touch his fore-arm.

His mind fizzed. The only way he was able to think about it afterwards looked completely stupid. He saw a sum in his head. He saw it so clearly that he felt he could have picked the figures and symbols up and moved them around, but he knew that as soon as he let go they'd slide back to the same place. The sum didn't mean anything. $0 - 0 + 0 = !$ That's all. But there was a sort of spinning excitement in the 0s, all possible possibles balancing each other out, meeting in the glorious explosion of the $!$,

which was like the largest of all rockets roaring away towards the sky, bathed in the flame of its thrust, turning gravity inside out with the sheer power of its take-off, so that it would never be able to fall back into nothing again.

In that fizzing instant James's hands knew the secret of the box. They had to pull and push at the same time, twisting in both directions at once, with a sudden little jiggle in the middle which had to come at exactly the right moment.

He did the pull-push and started the twists. He felt the box beginning to open, so he held it over the side and did the jiggle and finished the twists. It didn't open into two. It opened into *three*. That was the real secret. It seemed to spring apart in his hands.

He dropped it and leaned over the side to watch it fall.

BOOM!

Chapter 19

STAR-TREE

The explosion was so huge that it could have blown the world to dust. Only the hole ate it. The box must have fallen just far enough before it finished opening, so that the enormous force loosed itself into that enormous nothing.

Then there was silence.

Something funny had happened to time. James watched a millionth of a millionth of a second go by. He didn't need a clock or anything. Inside his mind he saw it happen, and had plenty of time to think about it. His mind was floating. The fizz the computer had put there, letting him understand how the box opened, was gone. Instead he had a feeling of pure light inside his head, like a perfect summer morning, dew sparkling on every blade of all the ideas that lay there waiting to be thought. The ideas were maths. You thought them with numbers, and they were beautiful. Now James understood why the computer had been so tiresome, not helping on the journey. It had to think about the box. It had to think immense and difficult sums and then make them balance all the way down to the sum with the three 0s and the !. Besides, if you could think like that all the time, you'd never want to do anything else.

Something touched his arm.

"Goodbye, James," said the Burra. "Thank you for coming. We could not have done it without you."

"Where are you going?"

"The Dump is starting to function. Look."

James turned his eyes towards the desert. Something was happening. The dunes, those vast, still ripples, had begun to move. They were sliding in towards the centre, falling in a roaring cindery torrent down into the hole of nothing over which the airship hung. The nearest circle was tumbling already. Half way down its slope, riding it like a surfer, was the explorer rat. It was only a black spot on the huge grey curve, but for a moment it was the centre of everything. It was standing on its hind legs, propping itself on its rifle, and holding its other paw up in the rat salute. It came like a hero.

"We have got to get there first, you see," said the Burra. "Goodbye, James."

It lifted its head off and chucked it over the side. Legs, arms and body leaped of their own accord. Everything was going. The basket plunged as the engine undid its bolts and rolled itself overboard. Only the computer was left, bleeping pitifully and trying to shrug itself along. It had always been so busy thinking it had never learnt to move. James picked it up and tossed it out. It fell with a burst of electronic hurrahs.

James leaned over the side to watch. Down below, infinitely deep into the blackness, things were beginning. The blackness had arranged itself into a whirlpool, a whirlpool without a whirl, like soup being liquidised in a kitchen mixer. Only the blackness wasn't coming back up the sides, the way soup does in a liquidiser, it was going on. Through. Beyond, to where a universe was being born. Stars and galaxies were streaming into existence like an upside-down firework display. An upside-down tree. They were fiery blossoms on the tree of darkness, all grown out of the box of nothing, in that million millionth of a second when it blew itself apart, subtracting its nothing from its nothing and dividing it by its nothing and making !.

The new universe was the !.

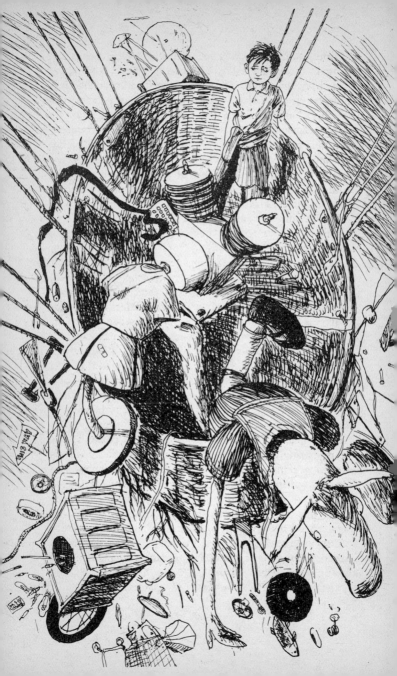

James couldn't use his eyes to see the stars and galaxies being born, because the light from them could never come back through the hole. Even light didn't travel fast enough. He saw them with his mind, blazing with the pure light of thought.

He saw something else too. It really had mattered, winning the race across the desert, because it meant the new universe was now going to be a Burra universe. He had no idea what that meant, or what a Burra universe would be like, but he knew that however it finished up there would be a sort of kindliness in its nature, as there had been in the Burra. Brave though the big rat was there was no kindliness in it. A Burra universe would be an odd sort of place, but it would be all right.

He looked to see where the rat had got to, expecting that it would by now have slid into the hole on its wave, but it hadn't. It was still in the same place, half way down the slope of the dune with the pouring cinders racing past it. It was like a solid ghost. The cinders seemed to be streaming through it and roaring over the edge without moving the rat an inch.

At first James thought this must be a trick of the moonlight, but it wasn't. He could see surprisingly clearly. In fact the night was becoming almost as bright as day. The moon was huge. Half of it was hidden by the gas-bag, but the other half was too bright to look at.

He turned his eyes away. Out on the horizon, above the marching grey ridges of the dunes, something glittered under the brilliant moon. Not stars, but a jagged line of brightness, where snow on the peaks of mountains reflected the moonlight. But he couldn't possibly see the mountains from here. They'd been out of sight for two days, below the horizon.

They were above it now. It wasn't only the dunes moving. The mountains too were churning in, sucked by the terrific gravity of the hole. Above their peaks the stars were growing brighter. They moved and jiggled, as if

James was looking at them through crinkled glass. As he watched, two of them collided in a burst of sharp white light, wincing bright. They had collided because they were moving in towards a central point and their paths had got too close to each other. So the stars were coming too.

The sun would be here before them. Somewhere below the earth it must already be spiralling in, and when it rose tomorrow it would fill half the sky, licking the earth with its outer flames, burning everything black. The sun was enormously bigger than the earth, and if the earth got too near it was supposed to crash into the sun and get swallowed up, but that wasn't going to happen. Huge as it was, the sun was going to be swallowed by the hole.

Before the sun, the moon. That was nearer still. James looked up, screwing his eyes almost shut against the brightness. He could see it both sides of the gas-bag now, and as he watched it grew bigger and bigger still, spreading and widening as it raced down, with the airship directly in its path.

Something moved beneath his hand where it clutched the edge of the basket. He looked down and saw that the airship was coming apart.

All this while—these few millionths of a second—the airship had simply hung there. When the rest of the Burra had thrown itself overboard with all its bits and pieces what was left ought to have shot into the sky because of losing so much of its load, but it hadn't. It was something to do with James being there and not belonging to this world. It was the same with the rat. The hole wasn't going to suck them in, or the things they were touching. But it was taking what it could. It was taking what the Burra called the "life" away—whatever it was that had made all the separate bits of rubbish agree to join up and become an airship. The actual part of the basket James was holding was really a bit of branch off a tree, as thick as a broomstick, left over from someone's bonfire. All the strips of old TV aerial and metal crate-ties and curtain rods and flex were unweaving themselves. The ropes that held the bag to the basket and the cords that made the net were losing their knots and unravelling. The bag itself was separating into the odd patches of plastic it had grown out of. As each piece came loose it flipped away down into the hole. In another few millionths of a second James was left floating in mid air with a branch in his hand, the great black gulf below, and the huge moon rushing down towards him.

He closed his eyes.

"I want to go home," he said.

Chapter 20

HOME

When James opened his eyes he was sitting in a conker tree, with his right hand gripping a living branch. The roaring was still there, loud but ordinary, as the bulldozers cleared the Dump level, getting it ready to turn into a park. Mum said that the Council had been promising to make a park here since before James was born. That was why they'd never cut down the tree. It was the one you passed on your way to school, just inside the Dump fence, before you got to the Nothing Shop.

James was gripping the branch as hard as he could because he was scared of falling. That was why he had shut his eyes, too. He wasn't usually afraid of heights, but he'd come too far out along the branch, trying to reach a conker, and the branch had started to sway and he didn't feel safe. He didn't dare move. He was stuck.

With half his mind James could remember quite well how he'd got here. He'd left home before the others to try and find a conker but the rubbish trucks had squashed them all so he'd wriggled through the fence, which he wasn't allowed to, and used the bars on its inside to climb up into the branches and then climbed higher and higher and worked his way out along a branch till it had begun to sway with his weight, and then . . .

But with the other half of his mind he remembered visiting the Nothing Shop and buying the box and Mum throwing it over the fence and him wriggling through the fence and finding himself on the far shore of an iron sea—and then the Burra and the airship and Rat City and the gulls and the race across the desert and the new Burra universe blazing into being while the huge moon rushed down towards him, and then . . .

. . . Then the two halves of his mind coming together again as he opened his eyes and found himself sitting in the conker tree. Both lots of things were true. Neither was a dream. But the one in the Burra world must have happened in a different kind of time, because he could still taste the after-breakfast toothpaste in his mouth. It was a pity he'd never be able to tell anyone about his Burra memory. They'd laugh at him and tell him he'd made it up or dreamed it. But he hadn't. It had all happened to him, James.

Thinking about it, and the things he'd done and endured on the Dump, far more dangerous than climbing a stupid tree, he felt ashamed of being frightened. He'd faced General Weil in his dreadful camp, hadn't he? He'd fought a duel with a great gull. He'd towed an airship across the desert. He'd started a universe off. He wasn't going to let himself get stuck in a tree.

He looked down. It seemed miles to the ground, but he forced himself to go on looking. The hard, pot-holed tarmac of the road was directly below him. In another gap between the big five-fingered leaves he could see a patch of bare earth inside the Dump where the bulldozers had finished scraping the ground level. He was wishing he was over that side because it looked softer to fall on when a large, dark rat scuttled into the gap, raised its head and looked boldly round. Its long whiskers quivered with interest and excitement. It didn't look frightened, though it must have been pretty bewildered by what the bulldozers had done to its world. Perhaps, James thought, it had two sets of memories too, one about the bulldozers and one about racing a strange airship across a desert. He hoped so.

Seeing it there, so brisk and brave, made James even more ashamed of his fright. He started to edge his way back towards the trunk. At once the branch swayed sickeningly and he had to shut his eyes and hold tight. He felt the whole tree was swinging to and fro, but after a bit he managed to open his eyes and try again.

He would have got down in the end, of course, without any help. It was sheer bad luck that Angie saw him. It was just like her, a totally useless kid, always mooning along and losing her gloves and tripping over things because she wasn't looking where she was going, but then noticing her brother stuck up a tree when he specially didn't want to be noticed.

The first James knew about it was Mum standing straight underneath him, with her hands cupped round her mouth, shrieking up through the roaring of the bull-dozers.

"Don't move! Hold on tight! I'll send for the Fire Brigade!"

She did, too. It wasn't bad, being rescued by the Fire Brigade, who came in a proper fire-engine with a red extending ladder that poked up between the branches, and a grinning friendly fireman who said it made a nice change from getting people out of burning buildings and used the ladder to pick the conker James had been aiming for. The fireman kept calling him "Sonny", which was a pity, but otherwise it was all right. And there was a photographer from the paper, too, except that a lot of other things happened that week so in the end they didn't print the picture after all.

It was even all right with Mum. It usually was when something serious happened. It was things that didn't matter she used to be boring about sometimes.

When everybody had gone away and they were tramping off to school with a twin gargling and the pram wheel twittering and Angie mooning along behind, Mum said, "I want you to tell me, James—I promise I won't be angry—but what on earth did you do that for?"

"I wanted a conker to go with my tree picture."

"Couldn't you find one on the ground?"

"The lorries had squashed them. Anyway, I wanted a whole one."

"It's a pity you decided to do a chestnut tree. It's a bit ordinary, don't you think? I bet that's what a lot of the others have done."

"No they haven't, and anyway, I haven't either."

James took the piece of paper out of his pocket. It wasn't as crumpled as he'd have expected, after all his adventures, but when he unfolded it he saw it wasn't the messy picture he'd drawn last night, watching the TV programme. It was the star-tree the Burra's pencils had helped him make in the cavern. And there were some circles on the back, too, which he'd drawn when he was trying to do the sum about how far it was to the centre of the dune-circles. That proved it, he thought. Not to anyone else, of course, but that didn't matter.

He showed the picture to Mum.

"Oh, that's pretty," she said, "though I wouldn't have known it was a chestnut tree. I suppose the stars are shining through the branches."

"It isn't a conker tree. I told you. It's a star-tree."

"Oh."

They walked on but she must have been thinking about it. They'd nearly reached the school when she said, "I still don't get it. If it isn't a chestnut tree, why'd you want to go climbing up for a chestnut?"

James put his hand into a pocket and pulled out the conker the fireman had picked for him. Carefully he levered the three sections open, teased out the glossy nuts and put them back in the pocket. He fitted the spiky green sections of shell together.

"I need an elastic band to hold it," he said.

"Am I being stupid?"

"It's a box of nothing, you see. Everything came out of nothing. That's what my tree means. The nothing is the seed, and it exploded itself into stars, and the universe started up."

"BOOM!" said Angie.